Edited by Maggie Helwig

# COMING ATTRACTIONS
## 00

We acknowledge the support of the Canada Council for the Arts, the Ontario Arts Council and the Government of Canada through the Book Publishing Industry Development Program for our publishing activities.

"Children's Chorus" by Christine Erwin was first published in *The New Quarterly* and "Blood Relations" by Christine Erwin first appeared in *Canadian Forum*. "Return Stroke" by Vivette J. Kady originally appeared in *Capilano Review* and "Soft Spot" by Vivette J. Kady was first published in *The Malahat Review*. "Francisco's Watch" by Timothy Taylor first appeared in *The Fiddlehead*, "The Resurrection Plant" by Timothy Taylor was originally published in *Canadian Fiction Magazine* and "Copper Cliff" by Timothy Taylor was first published in *The Malahat Review*.

ISBN 0 7780 1151 8 (hardcover)
ISBN 0 7780 1152 6 (softcover)

Cover art by Emily Carr
Book design by Michael Macklem

Printed in Canada

PUBLISHED IN CANADA BY OBERON PRESS

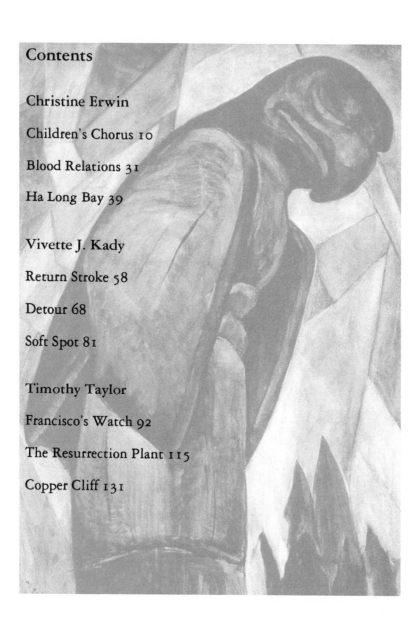

# Contents

Two of the writers in this year's *Coming Attractions* grew up overseas. Perhaps it is partly this that gives them their keen perspective on Canada and the world, and on human location and dislocation.

Christine Erwin grew up in Hong Kong, moving to Toronto when she was sixteen years old, and later worked as a librarian and creative writing teacher in Vietnam for two years. Her fiction has been deeply marked by her years in Asia. She writes, "Sometimes I think the most bruising and dazzling experiences of my life occurred before I was seventeen. Outsiders, whether they are immigrants, exiles, travellers or expatriates, make their way into my stories more often than not." Her stories can be surprising, disturbing—ruthless, in a sense, yet not without humour and compassion. "Take the night into me breath after breath and I'll be okay," says one of the narrators of "Ha Long Bay"; and so Erwin's fiction does.

Vivette Kady spent her early years in South Africa. Her characters, who range from teenage mothers to elderly dowsers, live dangerous and troubled lives, marked by miscommunication and pain, but also by intangible moments of joy. Indeed, it is perhaps those strange joys that are most vivid in her stories. "Lightning isn't just one single stroke that falls to the earth," says one of the characters in "Return Stroke." "It moves so quickly, we can't see it's actually rising, not falling." It is this rise in the midst of apparent fall that courses through Kady's work.

Timothy Taylor has already begun to make a substantial name for himself as a writer of fiction, though his first book has yet to appear. His characters live in a world of lost and missed connections, "an epoch of perpetual loss," as he writes in one story; and they cling to small objects—a watch, a dried root, a piece of property—as if they are the vehicles of grace which his people cannot be for each other.

Expect to hear more from all three of these exciting new writers.

MAGGIE HELWIG

7

Contributions for *Coming Attractions* 01, published or unpublished, should be sent directly to Oberon Press at 400–350 Sparks Street, Ottawa, Ontario K1R 7S8 before 28 February 2001. All manuscripts should be accompanied by a stamped, self-addressed envelope.

# CHRISTINE ERWIN

# Children's Chorus

It was several days before Marsha told Ford her premonition. She visited a fortune-teller and was reassured not with specific details, but with this: "The dreams are a gift." And it was this ring of information Marsha wore like a life-preserver, kept her buoyant; yet still she couldn't sleep certain nights, itchy with concern over what was going to happen. It was tempting to go back to the fortune-teller's table or another one, but would she be able to bear the truth? Before its chronological time? And besides there was the quandary of losing a year of her life every time she visited. In Chinese lore this was the price you paid for information of this nature. Wisdom unearned, she figured, or perhaps it was our lack of practice holding truth—an awkward and plain child.

Her night dreams, always plentiful, had changed. They were less and less about people who were familiar, and they seemed separate from her, as if they were arriving from somewhere else, another person's dream and were delivered to her by mistake. Like a postcard slipped into the wrong mailbox.

In one of her dreams...*A boy scratched out a ring in the dirt under the banana tree. Three marbles weighed down his pocket and he hoped to win more, hoped his friend was too busy with chores from his father to practise. Then, then he'd have a chance. The water buffalo lay nearby. A cord was knotted through its nose and one end looped back behind its horns. The other end lay under one back hoof, trailed a path to near the boy's hat. He'd set the straw hat down, out of the way, the better to see what he was doing, and besides, his hair was soaked with sweat, could dry this way. He took out his marbles and shot them. They jarred against one another. He loved that click when they hit.*

*He paused. He recognized the crunch sound. Boots. Then talk in that foreign language he'd tried to learn, even a few words, but soldiers laughed when he said anything. Nudged each other. Like these two soldiers now. He tensed. They were unpredictable when in small groups, but then he often found them mysterious. He couldn't* understand why they took to these dirt roads in the New Territories, why they were interested in the paddies and houses outside of Sha Tin village.

He pocketed his marbles for safekeeping, didn't want to give those up—there were no more where those came from unless he won them.

He dreaded catching their eye—it was as if they sensed this—he nonchalantly dug into the red dirt with his thumbnail. He reached for the rope, this end smooth from handling and then dared to glance their way. One soldier elbowed the other, and one pointed rudely at him. The boy bowed low hoping this would appease them, but there was no question they were calling him over. Best to play along, if he ran they'd come after him for sure. As he turned to his duty, the family's water buffalo, he misjudged his footing and tripped over the back leg of the animal.

The soldiers hooted. The animal started and majestically rose to its feet. The boy gripped the rope. He could hear the soldiers speaking to each other, nodding, roaring. The boy bowed to them again, looking from one to the other wondering if they were drunk and if so, what did that mean. For his chances.

Then one waved at him to come closer and in his haste he forgot his hat. He climbed onto the water buffalo, and in the slow unconcerned way of these animals, it started off in the wrong direction. It headed into the cool muck of the nearest paddy. The boy shouted, "Aiyaaa," to the animal (a term he would never use with it, but he didn't want it to head toward the soldiers). He slapped the side of the animal (not using his switch which was customary), shaking his head exasperated—he shouted back to them, throwing up his hands—he could tell they didn't know what to make of this. Was he deliberately defying them?—they stared at him, serious, unreadable. Suddenly, without thinking twice about it, the boy put his head down on the bony back of the animal and attempted a headstand—he'd slept on the beast before, but never this. The buffalo plodded on while he raised his skinny legs, and he saw the soldiers smile.

And then he heard his marbles fall: plop—the big one—plop, plop into the mud. Just when he thought he too would fall, his balance tottering, he saw the men turn and continue up the road. He was forgotten.

Marsha left Ford in bed, put on her silk dressing-gown and stood at their living-room window, the bank of windows holding all the lights of the colony. The reassuring sparkle from other people, other lives with down-to-earth problems. The harbour water was a mirror and also a kind of cradle; it held ships, one was definitely moving along. She was too far up the hill to see the wake but it was a sure thing. An absolute. No wake, no boat. These physical facts she fastened onto with the teeth of her mind.

She turned from the windows and drew out the piano bench. But then she remembered she'd left the bedroom door ajar. She couldn't play, it would wake him. And so she returned down the hall. She waited for Ford's chest to fall, watched him take his next breath. Reassured, she eased the door shut. With a sense of purpose, she lifted the piano lid. She cocked her head, her eyes following the lines of the instrument, the rack for music, the speech of this piano. She looked at the dull dark keys, the spaces between these and the white ivory keys. Yes, they were ivory. She wouldn't have bought it otherwise. If you lean over close to the keys, you can see the crisscross and cracks in the ivory; it means they are alive, were alive, not perfect. They were like a man's teeth, or perhaps his nails. You could see ridges. The light picked them out. She started at the high-note end of the keyboard, on the wood, and ran her finger across it—if you weren't slow and oh, so cautious yourself, you would miss everything, perhaps the piano would vanish—then glided across the ivory keys, filling each space with her finger, between, on to the next smooth key, thirsty with it, for it, closing her eyes, hearing nothing, feeling everything, agonizingly slow, note by note down the body of the piano to the final bottom note. But no sound. Bound to silence because people were sleeping, because it was night, because she knew the power of this piano, could play it with gusto while friends huddled around her Christmas scores stumbling out good cheer, riding the undercurrent of yearning for their families and snow and welcome back to their homelands. She knew the piano's voice, daytime singing—

she practised every day. Tonight, in the dark with only the outside lights and glitter, her fingers started up on the black keys, trailed up each key, up the middle white keys ...please. Let me know you like this. And after a time, with her left hand, she eased down a chord of notes, one note then another, no sound except a click or creak, the pressure of the wood yearning to spring back, like skin, and when she released her hand, the pads, the felt with a thwump returning to place. Like a tongue sinking back to its resting place in the bowl of your mouth.

Marsha boarded a liner for Vancouver at the last possible moment, leaving behind practically everything including Ford who was British (Ford would say Scottish) and who was thus registered on the government lists. She knew some wives were currying favours with officials in order to stay, saying it was cruel to tear apart families, saying they would volunteer in field hospitals should the very unlikely need arise, but Marsha made no such promises.

Ford sat forward in his chair spinning his ring, a gold one inset with a small Chinese coin. Marsha paced the living-room. If only she felt differently. If only she were someone else—a swashbuckling nurse, stoic, efficient, then she could bandage arms, she could soothe wounds or eyes or temples with cool, pristine hands. "But that's not the way I am. I'd feel like such a burden. I could sing for the troops." She shrugged. "Play the piano." She paused, studied him. "You probably wish I'd fight to stay, you probably wish I'd cut out my heart and give it to you."

"What do you take me for?" he'd said, sounding wounded. "It's actually something of a relief. I couldn't take care of you. Besides. You worry. It isn't going to happen. What would the Japanese want with Hong Kong?"

She'd shaken her head to herself, wanted to scream: It's not right, it makes no sense. Ford was too gentle. She was afraid he'd get crushed with an inability to kill. Her only hope was that the old four-legged part of him which acted blindly, physical survival, the force which surged through everyone, would save him.

Marsha packed the smallest of her floral suitcases with a week's worth of clothes. When Ford brought her a photo of himself, shyly held it out to her, she couldn't take it. If she took mementos of him, of their life here, it meant he would die. It would curse him in a way. Why would she need to keep the memory of him alive, why would that be necessary, if he was standing guard, his boots firmly on land. He came out of the bathroom with some jade jewellery—No. He suggested her piano music—Look, I'm coming back.

"Take something to practise," he said. "For me. Give me a private concert when this stupid thing blows over."

She flopped one piano book on top of her clothes and zipped the suitcase shut.

Ford took a scenic route around the Peak, and they drove past Mr. Wang's third and final unfinished mansion. It was to outward appearances more primitive than the other one, Eucliffe—an atavism. Uninformed people might have sworn it was an ancient walled village, or a battlewise fort which had protected Hong Kong from Portuguese pirates centuries ago. It was rotting; the plaster sinking behind grey lichen, the piles of sand and bricks sprouting bushes.

As they neared the harbour, Marsha searched for some significance in the halted construction and swift death of Mr. Wang. She wanted it to sum up her condition or the imminent attack. She wanted Mr. Wang's motto, "I love to build things," to carry some message. If you are not building, she considered, you are dying. Or are destroying. There is no middle ground.

Ford parked the car facing the water. It was deceptively calm within the harbour. She knew once the ship left dock, left Victoria Harbour in its wake, there would be nothing to see but swells, whitecaps, and that irritatingly simple line across the horizon.

He traced one of her blue veins from the crease in her arm down to her wrist. They were an innocent blue like ink. The faint lines made her look like a transparent fish, you could see the workings of her inner organs practically, skin and bones and heart.

He took the keys out of the ignition. She gripped his

thigh. "Listen to me," she commanded. "No matter what, whatever happens, if it comes down to a moment of life or death and, God forbid, you come that close, if you don't have the strength to live for yourself, live for me. Fight it. Do you hear me?"

The night Marsha's train shuddered to a stop at Union Station in Toronto, the windows were too steamed up for her to see anything clearly. She didn't stand up immediately, unlike the young couple in the next berth, swinging open the half wood, half dimpled glass door, letting the metal handle fly against the wall. The newlyweds, the man, knocked four times, rapidly, on her door. "Joy Keen," he hollered. She'd taught them to say goodbye in Cantonese. She hauled herself up out of her lower bunk and unlocked the door. They were charging down the corridor, hand in hand, but turned, beaming, and she waved. She expected jealousy to well up inside her, such youthful confidence, but what she drew was a blank. In fact, she was dazed by the distance between them. It felt like she was observing them through a viewfinder on the Peak.

She let her mother hug her as someone would allow another to hug a wooden telephone pole.

"This is everything?" her mother said. Such a worried, serious daughter, she'd almost not recognized her. She looked as if she'd aged fifteen years and immediately, instinctively, she felt angry at Ford: What was he expecting of her? What had he done? Worked her ragged? Not given her any fun at all? She would have said anything to Marsha in that moment, given her everything she owned (which wasn't much) but truly it took enormous control not to ask and say, Tell me. What has happened? Do you have news of the Japanese?

The snow swung at them, the windshield wipers barely able to fling back the thud—well, there should be a thud, Marsha thought, a bump from the soggy flakes colliding with the windshield—how could people string up Christmas lights already? Trying to force themselves and her into happiness. She dreaded her mother's effort to cheer her.

The snow dawdled. Stretched. Like a lazy aristocrat, it arrived unannounced and forced people to work harder; children liked it as a playmate, but from adults it demanded constant attention. It winked at her like shavings of glass. She scratched her forehead, skin tightening from the heat of the car. Stop making me like you, she wanted to yell out the window. It's the wrong time to be beautiful—I have worries, I have pains, things you know nothing of. Nothing.

Marsha's mother, Lil, willed herself on the drive and now as they strode to the stairs, not to keep touching her, or tease her—she is here, she is safe, nothing will happen to her, she would not let anyone hurt her, not here. Not in the safety of her apartment. Over her dead body, but with a terrible stabbing doubt knowing Ford had volunteered to serve. She knew what that very possibly could lead to, oh yes.

"How about I make us a pot of tea?" Lil said, a little out of breath. She unlocked the front door.

"How about something stronger?" Marsha dropped her bag and stamped her feet, the snow sputtering off her pumps.

"I've got sherry."

"Fine. At this point...." I'd drink kerosene, she thought.

"You and Dad used to drink it."

"Did we? Now where? I have two special glasses."

Marsha ran her hand through her hair. She'd forgotten after these years in the tropics how wet you got in Canada. Different. She remembered reading about the Eskimos. She called out: "Did you know the Eskimos have over one hundred words for snow?"

Her mother carried the etched glass cups past Marsha who was pulling out a dining-room chair, and said, over her shoulder, "Into the living-room." Marsha pushed the chair back in along its felt padded feet and followed. The chesterfield and armchairs were only a few feet away but it was her mother's favourite sitting area. She'd forgotten.

Marsha took the armchair. Her mother sank into the chesterfield, patted the empty place next to her. Marsha uncrossed her legs and moved next to her mother, tucking her feet under her skirt. Her mother took her hand—"Better," she said—then squeezed it. Marsha reached for the tumbler of amber liquid, and sipped it.

Her mother watched her.

They were silent. Marsha could not believe she was actually here in reaching distance of the afghans her mother knit.

"How could this happen?" she said, meaning how could she have stepped into the same position, the same scenario as her mother.

"I know."

"Is this some kind of joke?"

"There's serious talk of sending the Winnipeg Grenadiers. To support them. There's a troop in Vancouver."

Marsha snorted. "They're babies."

"Don't give up already," hissed her mother.

"Did you have any idea? An inkling with Dad? A premonition?"

"I put it out of my mind."

"I can't."

"It's the only way."

Marsha withdrew her hand from her mother's grasp.

"I remember when your dad...how he stood. So splendid in his uniform, a new haircut. Gleaming with oil. He was, he always looked clean-cut. Fresh."

Marsha didn't dare move. She waited, but her mother said nothing for awhile, her eyes darting back and forth as if following some scene in her head. And then she was back.

"It's not for sissies," her mother concluded.

Marsha wasn't sure if she was referring to war or memory.

Marsha lay in bed in the guest-room. She'd wanted to mention these dreams. They were not scary, but she felt weighed down as if she were meant to release them, act on them, but in what possible direction? The Japanese had not, in reality, invaded yet, but there was no question in her mind they would. On the one hand, she was apprehensive about what she'd see next, and on the other hand, the strange dreams were the only details she had access to. Canada was so far away.

She wasn't used to the hush of snow, to radiators keeping the rooms, especially the floors, at a human temperature through winter. The snow whirled on the other side of her window—the wind must have picked up because the flakes were spinning. If there was one snowflake there would always be another. While she drifted off, she wondered why the snow only tumbled down outside this window, her window, it hadn't come down from any other sides of the apartment. It was unnatural only this window could see it. This window with the venetian blinds drawn up showing her the snow....

*Horses. There were hooves, not a clatter but shifting, and not impatience simply the changing of position, shudder of skin to disturb flies. The somber straw covered the floor and the taut legs of horses seemed large, overwhelming. A dense smell of animal—musk joined with the sweetness of hay. The horses were tethered within a church, the sanctuary bright with sun finding the many windows, high arched with stained-glass pictures, patterns. Fans hung down from the ceiling. The blades spun lazily as if they had sense enough to keep an easy pace, why waste energy. Crying could be heard outside, a child perhaps, wailing. A man in a soldiers uniform, Japanese, sat on a pew. He was polishing his boots with a cloth, scraping mud or dung off the heel with a penknife.*

*He glanced up and saw the girl standing at the entrance to the church and continued with his boots. She did not want to walk across the straw floor in her bare feet, was afraid of what lay underneath it, so thick and piled up in places, scattered over the jumbled pews, many axed and burned for fuel. The rice bowl was warm in her hands, the heat soaking through the towel wrapped around the porcelain dish and lid. He snapped closed his penknife, uncrossed his legs and gestured with his hand for her to come to him. She looked at the forest of horse legs, and her feet crept toward him while pressing the bowl closer and closer to her chest—one of the horses shifted, suddenly and stamped his hoof so near her she started, and swallowed air. She clutched the rice bowl, the comfort of food which would not be hers, but his. And she ached with*

18

*hunger.*

*The man stood and patted the horse which had restless legs, sleepless eyes. He took something from his pocket and gave it to the horse. He took another sugar lump from his pocket, and came up to her. She thought he would let her eat it, a reward for delivering the meal. He reached for the bowl—unknowingly she held onto it—"Thank you," he said, in his language. She let go. He placed it on the pew and turned to her just when she was about to run away, and he pointed to the lump in his palm. Her mouth watered, and she swallowed, swallowed. He pointed at the animal with the huge head, and she understood what this man who her mother and sister and oldest brother said, if he or any of them come near you, you run, run as fast as you can. The soldier took her clenched, sweating hand, opened it and pressed the lump into her palm, rough, hard. And she stared at the sparkle, at the sweetness so close to her lips, mouth watering again. He lowered her hand moving to her mouth and pointed to the horse. And then he'd picked her up, she didn't like it. If she hadn't seen the horse's teeth the size of her fingers, steamy breath—how would the sugar get into its mouth? —she wouldn't have fallen back against him. He turned her hand over, and she studied the man's face. He clicked his tongue. Her palm open to the horse, she waited to be bitten. The snuffling of the horse on her palm, the startlingly fast lick or did it nibble? she wasn't sure, but the sugar disappeared. She kept staring at the horse, at the man, wishing she was the horse who got sugar. The ache in her belly was stronger than ever.*

*He set her down. She tore across the straw, glanced back once at him unbundling the cloth around the rice dish her mother had cooked. He didn't watch her leave, so intent on his food. And those horses who got to eat sugar. She charged down the stairs.*

*Her sister grabbed her hand: "Where have you been? are you all right?" She picked up the young girl. "Did he pay you this time?"*

*The younger girl shook her head.*

*"Bastard," she whispered.*

The narrow passage of stairs up to Sir Henry's bedroom in Casa Loma was always a hit with the schoolchildren. Marsha started her tour here even though Mrs. Wilson recommended the ground floor (the patterned wood floor, the

Italian marble), but Marsha wanted to grab their little attention spans right away. No child could resist a word when she lowered her voice as they passed through the panel door. Half-way up the steep stairs with her candle (Do you think it wise? Mrs. Wilson asked), she'd pause and request that the last child close the door. She could hear them breathing, fast, urgent. She'd inform them, slowly and in a sort of offhand way that Sir Henry planned numerous secret passages and hidden shelves and such, but alas, the plans, called blueprints, disappeared. Perhaps they were destroyed by the bank when he went bankrupt or by him in his anger. Or maybe he simply misplaced them, preoccupied as anyone would be completely out of cash. They were gone, and this staircase was all that had been found. So far. Or was there another? She would try to remember and tell them. But they must keep this in mind, to consider, where Lady Pellatt's diaries might be hidden, where the blueprints, rolled up and tied with a black ribbon, could be tucked away. In this way, she'd implant bits of history and architecture hoping some details would stick. She'd give them five to ten minutes in each room to knock along the panelling, the doorframes, the floorboards.

While in Sir Henry's bedroom she peered over the balcony to the gigantic foyer below, wondering why so big, and at the same time why could Ford not manage to squeeze a note, letter, something out to her. The Japanese Imperial Army was now in charge of Hong Kong, and Ford would be in a POW camp, probably at Sham Shui Po somewhere, but why had he not written? This silence was impossible to decipher and difficult to bear.

"I've found one," a boy shouted. "Mrs.... What's her name?" he whispered urgently to a friend. "Miss?"

Marsha crouched in the doorway with him and knocked on the molding. Several children gathered around them.

"See what I mean?" he said. And he banged higher up, then returned to the spot.

"Mmm.... Definitely a hollow sound," she agreed. She silently took out a spiral pad from her suit-jacket pocket, and because she could tell he would be disappointed with anything less than this, she licked her finger and flipped the pages to a blank one. She drew a rough sketch of the doorway and wrote the location. "Well-spotted," she said, borrowing one of Ford's expressions. The other children, she could tell, admired him in a way and were content to not ruin his elevation by clamouring for her attention.

On her way out that afternoon, Marsha tore off the slip of paper and handed it to Mrs. Wilson. "I'm not sure what I'm to do with all of these," Mrs. Wilson said, squinting to read it in the dark hallway.

"I know you sneak up there after I've gone, and pry off the panelling."

"I do not. You're teasing me, Mrs. Sinclair."

In fact it was Marsha who explored the corridors, wandered into barren rooms to fill her time after her tours were done. Time was something she dug into trying to diminish the pile rising around her, otherwise, she'd be buried alive. In one wing she knew there was an upright piano. She'd startled it when she peeked into the room. Or it her. The immediate charged pull, and she'd shut the door fast. Be quiet. It's impossible. But the piano ached and waited for her. Hung above her like a brooding storm cloud, or was it more like a shaft of light, illuminating. She wasn't sure.

She stepped out into the road, dry, thankfully. Moving into April and the mounds of snow were almost nonexistent. How endless the winter was and snow such an unperceptive guest. Never realized when it had overstayed its welcome. There was something ironic and painful about Mrs. Wilson collecting more notes and bits of information than she knew what to do with, while Marsha received no news at all.

After a few city blocks, she thought, if I'm important enough, if he truly loves me, he'll get a message to me. Somehow. What to someone else might appear a gamble, placing her past eight years on the table and saying, if I don't hear, then it wasn't real, to Marsha was reassuring. An obvious expectation. It was the least love could offer.

Another night. Another dream. The dreams disturbed her

yet she craved them, they were all she had. *It was awkward for the boy to see out the window, not simply because of the wrought iron grillwork, but because his mother's three lines of laundry were strung up in front. It was their family's window; the boy claimed it by opening and shutting it when he felt like it. A luxurious possessive gesture. It didn't make any difference what kind of weather was outside because the glass was broken before they arrived. His mother had dug out the jagged pieces.*

*He stooped under a towel and stood pressed against the windowsill, sticking his arms out through the bars, hanging them out in space which belonged to everyone and no-one. This action was not allowed. Nothing was. But he was prickly hot from the beach, and besides, their weekly visit was over, and now he had to wait another week. He rocked on his heels back and forth. If he could stay here at his post—he liked to think that way—long enough he'd see the twilight descend. The front steps of their civilian camp, used to be called St. Stephen's College, would darken. The concrete would appear to be all the same colour. Same dark. The bats flitted drunkenly between trees; these creatures which had unnerved him at first, were now companions he waited for each evening.*

*He snapped his fingers. He wished more than anything else for a sheet of paper. Even a newspaper, any scrap, so he could get down on one knee, fold it in half, run his finger down the fold line, twice. Then opening it out again, the corners would rustle because there would be a slight breeze. To carry his plane. Then each top corner folded into the centre, perfectly aligned—his tongue popped out of his mouth as he considered the careful folds—then creased toward the centre again. Must be careful with the nose, not to bend it, keep it pointed. Then he'd return to the window where he stood now, and he'd send it out. It would fly, graceful, cradled on the air. Safe.*

*"John...John come away, love."*

*And his plane would land without a bump or bang, smooth— he glided his hand exactly as it would touch ground—far away from the eerie blood stain on the stairs, the brown smears down the walls of this classroom.*

*His mother caressed his ankle, reaching for him from her sitting position on the blankets.*

*These blood stains—he'd studied them endlessly—looked like*

22

*countries. Or new continents adrift, unconnected to the world he'd known; the globe he'd spun in his father's study. They were unnamed and barren.*

Some nights it took a while to fall back to sleep and tonight Marsha thought back to the boy, John, did she recognize him, no, no and not his mother...the college, yes, once she'd substituted there as a music teacher, but aside from that brief stint, there was nothing else familiar in the dream. No light, no understanding beyond watching a kind of personal and private documentary.

On her way down the hall to the kitchen, she noticed her mother's light was on. She knocked tentatively, considering she might simply have fallen asleep while reading. Her mother answered, and Marsha offered her a cup of hot milk since she was heating one for herself. "Love it," her mother said.

Marsha found a pot, smelled the milk.

"I just opened it this morning," her mother said, startling Marsha with her presence.

"Sneak."

While Marsha stirred the milk with a wooden spoon, her mother shook open the buffet drawer and took out a box of matches. Her mother was preoccupied with collecting candles. She had Easter ones, Christmas angels, candelabra to fill, and Marsha expected to see her take out the short brass candlesticks and everyday white candles. She was astonished to see her mother draw a pack of cigarettes out of her dressing gown pocket.

"Close your mouth, dear."

"Since when have you smoked?"

"Nothing to worry about. There's lots of things"—her mother smirked, mischievously—"you don't know about me."

"And whose fault's that?" It came out before she'd known what she'd said. Marsha was embarrassed she'd commented at all. She dipped her baby finger into the opaque milk, then popped it in her mouth. It shocked her, still, how stupid her mother could make her feel sometimes.

"This is wonderful," her mother said, taking a saucer from the cupboard for the ashes, and following Marsha into the living-room. "Such a treat!"

"I'll have one, then," said Marsha. She lit up. "I'm having dreams. Tonight I had one. They're odd. I don't know how else to say it. They're just odd."

"What did we have for dinner?"

"I don't think it's that."

Marsha's mug was turning cold in her hand while she rested it on her leg, and she set it on a coaster.

"I think it's really good you keep busy. I think that's wise. I only wish I could have known you'd be back because I would never have lent out the piano."

Marsha shrugged. "I'm not in the mood. Do you want more—"

"But you're a concert pianist. The years. You must be losing your mind."

Possibly, Marsha thought. Very possibly.

"Maybe you could use the one at the church. Why don't we talk to the new minister? Brian Hodder. I think that could be perfect. That's what we'll do."

Marsha cleared her throat. "You're bossing me, mother."

"Am I?" Her mother drew out another cigarette, she offered one to Marsha. "I'm just"—she took the light Marsha gave her—"trying to help. I feel terrible I didn't have room in this apartment, but you know I didn't give it away. I lent it."

"You didn't cause any of this." Perhaps it was sitting in the semi-darkness which gave Marsha courage, or maybe a hunch that the simplicity of hot milk with pyjamas could not foster lies or evasions. Nothing would be held against anyone. "Mom? Am I like him at all? Like dad?"

There was a long tense silence. And then a big sigh. Marsha held in check her desire to rush in and say, "Forgetit forgetitforgetit."

"Sometimes you come out with a line and you sound exactly like your dad. It's amazing. The way you pull someone's leg, there's something you do with your chin, drop it,

I think. Startles me, even now. It's nice." She paused. Then, she stood. "That's enough of that," she said, not unkindly.

Her mother leaned forward and gathered the handles of the two mugs in one hand. She slipped the pack of cigarettes back into her dressing-gown pocket. Marsha heard the clatter of the mugs as they were placed in the sink. She couldn't help feeling as if her father had died twice. The memory of him would end with her mother—closeted as if he'd never existed. And yet it was obvious all sorts of things were going on in her mother's head—reminders, echoes. Marsha was walking evidence.

When she was younger and asked questions about him, her mother stiffened, looked angry. Somehow Marsha sensed her mother wondering why she was focusing on who wasn't there. On the hole. But it was, she realized now, to decipher the dimensions. To see if she was big enough to fill it.

She was not. She was the wrong shape. She was somebody else.

Marsha took out the music book she'd brought over from Hong Kong and studied the notes as if they were Chinese characters, unfathomable. Only the highly educated, the special, the deserved had access to them. She tried playing the right hand, the tune, tapped it on the pages lying open across her lap, imagining middle C, the piano—folding her thumb under her fingers to move up to higher notes, humming the tune. It was most definitely not as satisfying as the instrument, the smooth keys like satin, and although she ached for it, there was a pleasure in the want. Failed, unfulfilled want. She should suffer too. Ford was. She'd left him after all, perhaps if she'd stayed they'd be in a camp together. Who knows? Some of her friends, no doubt, were locked up.

This was a way to atone. She used both hands with the score shoved along her knees. If there was such a thing as two-dimensional music, this was it. Like singing without opening your mouth but that, of course, was humming. What was fingering out a bar, a line of a song without sound, without a piano or harmonica or any ear-filling satisfying noise? Was there even a name given for that? She finished an entire concerto—the timing tricky. It ended up sounding like a single melody line. No matter how many fingers came down at once, there was no depth, no chords. Someone listening wouldn't hear, as she did, the many notes high and low, rising tension—her pushing harder on the book. The page, the book didn't give the way the piano keys did, didn't respond like her living, breathing piano which was probably smashed to bits by looters. Or stolen. She stopped. Shoved the book into the bottom of a pile of paperbacks, newspapers and war bulletins.

You didn't get awards for survival, for commonsense. Yes, she surrendered before anyone else, she gave in to life and ran like hell. Pell mell, as they say. It was hard for her not to wonder though, if Ford was naive, knowing about her father, knowing the past and still explaining to her in a suffocating voice where his duty lay.

Meanwhile, she'd sat bolt upright on the other side of the rosewood coffee table. "Stop talking at me in your checklist voice. I'm not an irate customer at the bank. If you're under some mistaken impression this fight, this— I'm telling you it's going to happen—a war, that there is some logical, justifiable reason for it, you're a fool."

He talked faster, "It's necessary to defend the colony, defend the Chinese, everything we've built here."

She leaned back. Weary. She stared up at the brass light fixture with punched out holes such that at night the light speckled the walls and tile floor. She didn't know how to reach him. "Let the Chinese," she paused, they'd discussed this before, "defend themselves and their families."

"You know I have no say. We have no say."

A handful of trusted Chinese were to be given arms, the rest of the population, over a million, were protected only by the label, civilian. What was the worst, Marsha thought, was how the Governor and even her friends talked as if there were no choices, as if the situation as it stood was inevitable and unavoidable.

He leaned forward in his chair, elbows on his knees.

"They need me. I have no choice, Marsha."

"What about Bruce Potter?"

He rolled his eyes. "Come on. He's a loose cannon. Got nothing to do with principles. He thrives on being an obstacle."

"You barely know him."

"More than I care to. He's not a good example." He stared at the floor for a moment. "I can't walk away from this."

She remembered then, how she felt when she used to go to her piano. How she'd forget him, the time, how the hours would disappear as if cut out by invisible scissors. How it was difficult to reconcile that sometimes she chose, preferred to be away from him. Not because she cared for him less, but because the piano was hooked to her pulse, had become essential to her many lonely years before. There hadn't been a price to it before. Nothing at stake. It was ironic now that she lumped the two together Ford and her music.

*Then the girl caught sight of what she'd been yearning for: a crab. And not a young one, but with a shell as big as her hand; this was what she would bring back for dinner. She leapt off the rock, avoiding the bone white barnacles, and watched the crab scuttle into a crevice. She sat on her heels, peered in. She could wait, it would come out eventually. Climbing higher to watch the hiding place from a distance, she startled a gull. It circled and landed on a rock not far off. Sitting, she glanced at her family's sampan, her anchor, then looked up behind her at the foliage not as green as earlier in the year. Dense and entangled. Above the leaves, high up the hillside, she could make out the castle and the lampposts. The Japanese army lived there, had taken it over and she didn't want to go anywhere near nor have the soldiers catch her eyeing the building.*

*She leaned forward, looking down for the crab. Not out yet. Then she turned to her left. Scanned the rocks on the other side of her.*

*She sprang up. Backed away. It took a few seconds for understanding to seep in. Afraid to turn her back, but more afraid to stay, she sprang down to a lower boulder, her bare foot smarting on the rock.*

*"Maaaa!" the girl screeched, and her father stood, fishline in hand. She saw his eyes searching the scrub behind her, scanning the rocks.*

*"Someone's fallen," she cried over and over, pointing.*

*Reassured by her father's hand, she retraced her steps over the rocks. The surf spat up beside them, the barnacles popped and clicked. She stopped abruptly and took her hand out of his. Her father's face closed as he climbed over the last rock, the way it did when he encountered soldiers in the harbour. And because he was dealing with it, must know what to do, she ventured up the boulder. He moved cautiously toward the European in uniform, his eyes prowling the area. He scanned the water, the bay, his eyes climbed up the bank to Eucliffe castle. Satisfied of no immediate danger, he grabbed the belt and rolled the man onto his front. It was then she saw the stiff eyes, the huge dark stain and open wound. And flies. Her stomach convulsed.*

*Afterwards, she wiped her mouth wanting to rid her tongue of the caustic, invasive taste. Her father's black hair fell forward, long bangs, as he leaned over, murmuring as if he were talking to the dead European. He gripped the wrist, hesitated, and it was then she saw a glint, a ring. A coin inset in gold catching the morning sun off guard. Her father yanked it off. He pulled out his folded handkerchief from inside his trousers, opened it to where there used to be a wad of bills and some coins, but now, and for some time, there had been nothing. He placed the ring on the cloth, neatly flicked the corners of the handkerchief over and tucked it back inside his waistband.*

*Somehow he managed to lift the European, take his arms and heave him up to his shoulders. A cloak of stone. Unsteady, his knees bent, he dragged the big man over the rocks. She could hear her father's breath heavy, laboured and then, with an escaped grunt, he half-hurled, half-dropped the man into the ocean. There was a deep splash.*

*She watched her father wash his hands, wash his arms to the elbows in the ocean. "The sea is the best we can give him," he said, grimly. It was when he stood and beckoned for her to go with him back to the sampan that she balked. She hesitated, looking for no known reason at the sinking body.*

*He came back to her with a curious expression on his face as if to say, You waste your heart on a stranger? Hers were not tears of sadness though. He cupped her cheek in his hand, but she would not look up at him. Why had her father not spared her? Taken care of this somehow before she'd stumbled upon it? Of what use was he, if he could not save her from such horror.*

Awake, Marsha didn't move. Her head was unusually clear, and she was convinced if she could hold this overwhelming awe of death just a few seconds more, displayed before her would be the wisdom of the ages.

She remembered the moment of her father's death—safely home, at last, with one leg, and him crashing down the stairs. Stunned by the act, stepping to the side as if he wasn't her father, she was spellbound by the mystery of where he had gone. His chest still. His breath missing.

A sparrow peeped. The sun bloomed quickly, she noticed, once it began. Like a bubble surfacing from underwater; it seemed to speed up when it neared the barrier between sky and lake.

Marsha knew exactly where the room was in Casa Loma just like an animal knows the location of the nearest watering hole. She stood there in the empty room beside the piano. She studied it, afraid it would bite her, accuse her of some abandonment crime, a kidnapping of its voice box, holding back the notes. She was relieved the piano had so few demands: only to be touched, allowed a voice, to sing. She raised the cover of a weathered, but familiar friend. The tops of some keys were chipped, all were nicotined yellow. One black key was gone.

Play, she told her fingers hanging on the edge of the piano, the tips sunk in the dust beside the ivory road. You have to. You must. And because the piano longed for them, they raised themselves up, and one finger played a key, a black key, and hit it again softly, then again and again, faster, harder, more fingers, crashing down, anything, any notes, the piano creaked and wheezed with lack of use, the strings out of tune increased their ranges and there seemed to be more notes than ever before, she smashed her palms down, discord and rage flying, her palms stamping down the keys, Break, Break, she muttered and she clenched her teeth. You're not going to be able to withstand me. I have more fight than you can imagine; but the keys did not collapse, except for one which suddenly stopped playing, the strings snapped.

Her hands hovering, she paused. She wiped her nose with the heel of her hand.

I could...I could...she tried to imagine the worst possible thing, the most horrible, sickening thing to do to this instrument, which was the world, her world, which could allow and carry such hate—fire? an axe? peel it apart piece by piece?

Her lower back ached from standing and pounding. She massaged it, slow and thoughtful, then leaned forward again, each elbow on three keys, head in her hands. Face to face with one who would not be lied to. The discord of the notes faded out of earshot. Nothing and everything pressed on her at the same time.

# Blood Relations

My mother did a slow headstand directly after intercourse with my father, not because she was lightheaded, but to be sure she would give birth to a girl. She also waited until the absolute last minutes of her difficult labour before settling on the name Joan rather than Jill. Her care paid off. Pleased and stunningly exhausted, she lay back in her cranked up hospital bed, asking the staff to please let her see me. No, she wasn't too tired. She took one look at me bundled up in the nurse's arms and said, "That's not my baby. Look. Look at her yellow skin. That's a Chinese baby."

Already, from day one, my identity was under question, under scrutiny as if my mother had do-se-doed with an Asian man, unknowingly, or perhaps my skin and bones had unearthed some recessive gene in what everyone assumed was ancient Scottish stock. Stolid. No-nonsense. The nurse passed me to my mother and in reassuring tones explained about my blood. Bad blood, it turns out.

The different blood of my parents would not mix in my house of flesh. The strains wouldn't join harmoniously without lumps, would not nourish each other into a deliberate, glossy swirl. No. They fought. They struggled within me, and if my newborn blood was not immediately drained out the bottom of one foot (such small feet for an inhuman tube), and a fresh batch of a stranger's blood pumped up through the other foot, I would die. My blood cells were in civil war creating a bile potent enough to alter the shade of my skin.

Who was this woman whose blood I received, the one who discreetly took part in the blood drives which toured the downtown offices on weekdays? I've got all sorts of theories: an airplane pilot, an electrician, a distant relation of Gandhi. With my luck, it was a guy, a very male guy with heaps of body hair. (A characteristic which will be passed on, no doubt.)

It was probably nobody important.

But what's key here is not simply the blood, it's the race

I was mistaken for because, you see, I should have arrived between the legs of an Asian woman. There was most definitely a mix-up. I belonged in China. To China. And by some cruel twist of fate had arrived in London, Ontario.

When I was five I would eat nothing but rice. Rice until I threw up not knowing enough to stop when full, when the belly had expanded to capacity because I seemed to not trust I would ever have this staple for my blood again. My father relished rice like me, my mother demanded pared boiled potatoes. My mother would encourage me to dribble soy sauce onto my rice, but my father would snatch the leaky bottle and shout I was to add only butter. This back and forth, this yin and yang; it confuses the blood. I could hear it welling up in my head, surfing, roaring, crashing down the arteries then sucked back up my veins like an uncontrollable tide.

You think I'm exaggerating? You think I embellish the facts? I wish I was a storyteller, a bard in the Scottish tradition, but I am of Chinese heritage. I tell you the truth or am silent. Oh, I may sweeten words to flatter you, yes, to please you, but about things of importance like family, the passions, I would never lie. Cowardly.

In later years at school, I asked my friends to call me Faith. I like names to have meaning, to hold in each letter the strands of pictures, stories, and with a name like Joan, what does J-O-A-N mean? There was Joan of Arc. The young woman who, after saving her fellow citizens from invasion, was burned from the feet up. Reading between the lines, you can tell they thought her ego was as big as the sun. And as calm. Once she was buried, people said they felt badly, maybe they'd overreacted.

My blood has never been shared. I have never given any away in Red Cross drives, have never allowed an ounce to fall without licking it back into circulation. I cannot spare a drop. I want it to be as pure as possible; I want it to increase and fertilize every inch of me. When you've almost died and then survived a complete overhaul, you need to hold tight, clasp your own because certainly no-one understands, no-one can understand how it is to be Chinese as I know I am but not look Chinese. I can't even wink with almond eyes. It's a punishment.

When I asked for moon cakes for Christmas because I'd learned from Lucy Cheung, my best friend at school, that she loved them, I was presented with a cake pan shaped like a star and a cake-mix box. My mother said she'd tried, but there were no nail-clip half-moon tins. She hoped I'd make it from scratch. My father said that with the cake-mix he'd bought me, I'd have it in the oven in no time. And if I wanted a full moon, why not simply use the 9" round cake tins in the cupboard.

"Thank you, parents," I said in Cantonese. I was learning discipline and reserve. I think I was also beginning to feel superior to them. This would be my downfall.

Lucy told me her blood was northern Chinese blood which had crossed the seas, costing her grandmother her every possession. They fled the Communists and made a new life in Hong Kong. The city of lights, Lucy called it. But too hot. Also people spit, and she faked it, her chin jutting forward, the blue veins in her neck apparent under her yellow skin. Actually not yellow, creamy, a rich colour. In summer she was caramel.

In Grade 6, I was caught whipping a snowball with a rock inside at a boy named R.B. A pig's fart. A stupid overweight boy with too much lip who had called Lucy a Chink. It was interesting he hadn't called us both that, and I suspect this offended me as much as the smear of pleasure on his face. He was an easy target; he could barely run, more like waddle. I got him when he turned to see how close behind I was, nailed him in the side of the face. The rock drew blood.

"Tell R.B. you're sorry," the vice-principal said, "and we'll go from there." (This was her statement which meant things will be better for you if you do as you're told.)

"I didn't mean for your blood to come out," I said, quietly. If I had to look into his smirking face any more, I was going to have to hit him.

There was some silence. "You have an unusual way of putting things," she said. But left it at that. I was to write lines that evening something like, I will not throw snow-balls in the schoolyard because someone could get hurt. Instead, I wrote her an essay: The Nature of Blood and Colour. I wrote endlessly, I believe it went on for twenty foolscap pages, both sides. The longest essay I'd ever composed, at least that's what my teacher, Miss Bell, said.

My main point (and I did have some knowledge in this area because I'd done a lot of reading in the public library down the block from city hall) was your blood determines your outlook, your skin, your tastes, and even the supposed myth of royal blue blood has certain basis in fact. I mentioned, of course, my birth and how unavoidably—I certainly didn't blame my mother or father for this—I'd been stolen from a village in China near Beijing called Chulu well-known for its lacquer art. My blood father spent long days working while the lonely wind of northern China weaselled its way into the factory. Many of his colleagues died from the fumes of the lacquer; it was a dangerous occupation—more dangerous certainly than office work of a dubious nature which my other father was very busy at. He could not find any free time. (Find as if it were misplaced like car keys, lost forever like my real blood parents.) This particular man in China, I suspected his name was Wang Mu (a name I'd found in a book and which I could pronounce with aplomb), but I didn't know for certain. He had one son at home with his wife, my true mother, Sarah. She was half-white, the daughter of a missionary to China. But there was a boy. I had a brother. I was not meant to be an only child. Yet he was feverish, unaccountably ill. Something in his blood, I think. (This was the weakest part of the story.) Anyway. My mother made fried rice and crispy noodles (both!) every day. She was waiting in the shadow of the low doorway, just inside their house, for when I would arrive as some day I would. I must. She would have a thick braid down her back and would teach me proverbs, or would recite legends of the mountains. While we waited for the air to cool down enough to sleep, she would sing Chinese rice planting songs. She would not shoo me out of the kitchen with a "Finish your homework, honey. Now." She would not cry so much. She would not be forever sending me to the end of the street for more stupid potato chips. Potatoes. Potatoes. Potatoes. I wanted Peking duck.

I went on in that vein for a bit, doubtless I had no idea what I was saying. The single person I'd told about my mother threatening to leave my father was Lucy, and she said there was no such thing as the D word in Chinese families.

I remember how sometimes I'd stay on the school bus and go to Lucy's apartment, ride the elevator to the twenty-seventh floor. Her place was always full of people, of dark ornate furniture, of nutty smells. I'd swim through the blue and green beads hanging in the kitchen doorway and watch her mother light the small Hibachi barbecue resting on bricks on the floor. This way, Lucy explained, they could eat charred drumsticks and marinated beef all through the winter. She showed me the bedroom she shared with her mother and her older sister. The three of them slept in the same double bed. "My mother snores," she said in my ear, as if her mother could hear this confession while she fanned the coals in the kitchen. "My sister pinches me in bed. I pinch her back. We kick each other to not laugh and wake my mom."

Lucy's father was employed in a soap and perfume factory. Most of the time when I was there he was asleep in his bedroom. He worked night shifts, her mother, the day shift, sewing. Her older sister and her grandmother were the people Lucy counted on. Once in a while Lucy would bring me potpourri beads her father had brought home, or else bath soaps carved like lacquer ware into roses or shells. "Your father is lucky," I said, imagining him stirring vats of soaps, pouring them into moulds the way my mother used to tip her mixing bowl and pour batter for cupcakes.

She frowned. "In Hong Kong? He was a teacher. In Canada, they don't want him to teach."

"Why?"

She shrugged.

"Who?"

She tapped her bedroom window. "Them."

35

I didn't know what to make of it, of that sort of information, so I tucked the barb away. I put it where I was shelving lots of things, confusing things which mattered but I didn't know how or why. As long as I knew where they were hidden, I could keep the mess at bay, it could live in me. I knew I could count on myself.

When Miss Bell called on me to stay behind after class, I figured it was about the China I knew and loved so well. Perhaps she didn't want to believe in it, perhaps she couldn't fathom that the teas my Chinese mother brewed for Liu, my brother, had such miraculous powers, and that a daily dose of ginseng root was so important, or that the Tiger Balm rubbed onto his chest helped him breathe. He was getting better in China, soon he would return to school, put on his uniform, blue shorts, white shirt and bring pride to my parents. There was much expected of him.

Miss Bell, with a dramatic sweep of her hand, said it was a brilliant story, but she wondered about the divorce part. Which? I wondered. Oh, that part. I held my breath because it felt like a mistake to hear it. But I hadn't shot the word into the air between us like a bullet. The word had dripped onto the page and into my essay, had flowed out naturally like the Yangtze River to the East China Sea.

Bad blood. Bad mixture. There are people who don't get on, my mother explained later, they create a poison together—A pus? I interjected—yes, it's not intentional, but it is part of their manner. I considered to myself that one of them should be drained, cleared out. Remove their old blood and pump in a new batch. You could choose the donor maybe. You could ask for a farmer's blood; someone who is methodical and patient. Someone who is content to stay home and watch plants grow.

"It's all right," Miss Bell said, in a faraway voice. "I'm not angry with you."

You can't take back words. They fly out and they are no longer yours, they belong to everyone. In China, I know, it's dangerous to say some things out loud. You have to be cautious. I was working on reserve. I was trying hard to keep dangerous words close at hand so I knew where they were. The risk is they might cut you. They need to be handled with care. It wasn't so much pain I worried about, it was that I couldn't spare the blood. Mine was irreplaceable. And if new blood was added it might contain argumentative or quirky characteristics.

I concentrated on Miss Bell's bangle that afternoon. It was a deep red lacquer one which Lucy gave to her at some point. I wanted it to be mine. (Perhaps my blood father had carved the design.) It should have been mine, the chrysanthemums, the peacocks, the shine. The inside smooth, smooth, wanting to take my tongue to the inside, to feel a surface free of knobs and obstacles. It takes hundreds of applications of the paste on wood before it is ready to be carved. Layer upon layer, allowing each one to dry before the next. And every carved petal of the peony or curve of a plum, each meaning more than just a flower or piece of fruit. A plum, for example, blooms in the face of winter and this is why it means hardiness. And individuality.

"Does your stomach hurt, Joan?"

"Faith," I said.

I'd been hugging my waist unawares. My hands pressed it, furious. My blood was rioting inside me like my brother's in China, the fighting from within. I'd hoped if I ignored the gnawing, it would stop. But by now it was constant.

I was kept in hospital for a week while they once again pumped foreign blood inside of me. My stomach had been acting up, chomping away at itself, at the lining and the ulcer was far along. The nurses were kind, and the doctor joked around with me, slipped me jujubes faster than you can say, "Kung hei fat choi."

"What's my fortune?" I asked him.

"You're fortunate to be alive."

And I wanted to add, But will I live to be a hundred? Will I wear a brocade jacket? Will I always have red blood to ride the days of my life?

My mother and father came to the hospital—the last time I've seen them arrive anywhere together—and I thought having the two in an enclosed room would send the metal beds crashing into each other, that the pale walls would cave in, and the nurses, justifiably, would herd us out for disturbing the peace.

My mother turned my hand over, and with one finger, began a tingling swirl on my palm. My father sat on the other side of the bed cupping my knee like it was a baseball. I think he didn't know what to say either. "Are you tired?" he said suddenly.

"If I close my eyes," I said, "I could fall asleep." And then I regretted saying it because he left right away, and I hadn't meant it like that.

"Close your eyes," my mother whispered.

Lucy wanted to give me a gift at the end of the school year, something to remember her by. I hadn't told her yet my mother planned to move to Anywhere But Here, Lucy just seemed to know. Chinese astrology? Bamboo fortune sticks? Intuition? She pressed me to say what I wanted.

My hopes were high. Something I'll have forever. That I can never lose or have taken away, thrown out in a mother's cleaning binge. Something I can carry with me always. A gift pure Chinese.

"Is this a riddle?" she said.

I knew what I wanted and I was afraid she'd refuse me because she could, she had every right. Something I will never have to explain to anyone, or prove, or confess because it will be only for her and me to know, until death. Until we meet again in the next life on the Great Wall.

"I want some Chinese blood."

She got up, and without a word, rushed out of her bedroom, and I understood her reaction. I'd never wanted to give away even a drop of my own precious blood. Blood keeps you alive. Without it you are nobody, nothing more than a potato. Lucy came back into the room holding up a pin.

# Ha Long Bay

## DENIS

I tuck the wood—wrist-sized branches about the length of a woman's arm, fingers broken off—under my arm. There's a path behind the government hotel and it leads up the hill over the pass and down to the beach, one of two, below. We were going to collect the wood, hike through the bush. Like back home. But our tour guide urged us to buy a few bundles from the locals. I was pissed off actually, I'd looked forward to scouting in wilderness. Perhaps I needed to face the nagging fear of land mines and unexploded bombs. I think I wanted some dark danger. Wanted to push myself up against a fault line and feel as close as she must have, the spark of terror before she blacked out.

We need, I figure, something excessive tonight. Build and burn. That's why I suggested a fire to the others while we were in Ha Long Bay. It popped into my head in the cave, the hideout for children—Gateway to Heaven—used during one or many of the wars. I had no idea, but I should have, there were so many altercations in this country. The American War, they call it here. Top billing for us. You can bet it took a few months for me to get my head around that.

I hope this stuff burns okay. I wonder if Esa's bundle is any dryer—this humidity is a pain in the neck.

Maggie and Kate are walking ahead: Kate paying close attention to her feet, Maggie asking questions about Kate's boil on her lip. Induced by stress and/or tiredness, I hear. Esa is a few steps behind them when we start the climb up the hillside, and I'm further behind still. The gravel slides and protests under us, but even in this pitch black, we manage okay. At the top, the crest of the hill, there will be a house, gatehouse, you could call it, and a toll. A few thousand dong, I think. I sincerely doubt anyone will be manning it this late, almost ten o'clock, but then what do I know?

When I was at the top earlier today, a skink caught my eye. I inched closer, and then realized I was face to face with a pillbox set into the cliff. Where's the door? I wondered. Finally, I gave up the search and guessed there was a hidden tunnel. They're big on tunnels. I've seen lots of pillboxes, quiet as eyes, on this island. When on the boat, too, I picked them out on a scatter of islands in the bay. We anchored, at one point, at an isolated beach to swim, and the guide showed me mussels he'd chipped off the rocks. He said they were good in soup. I figured we'd connected in a way, and so asked him if these concrete outposts, especially the ones near the town of Cat Ba, were from the American War. He shook his head. "French," he said. "Many years." He returned to breaking off shells. I felt oddly disappointed as if it would have suited me better that they were prepared for American attack; to appease me in some way, to see in solid form their cleverness and strategic abilities. Perhaps he feared offending me and wished to downplay our pocked influence. I didn't believe him, in truth.

I think a fire is a good elemental thing. Something to look at. Something familiar to the four of us in this foreign land, and it might comfort. Food is the best thing for grief, and I'd be happy to cook if I could find a kitchen counter higher than my knees.

Esa shifts his load while we contemplate our climb down to the beach.

Maggie fiddles with her waistband—"Eeek," she mutters. "I don't want to go headfirst."

Nobody speaks for a moment. I shift the wood to my other arm. Then me, I say, "Let's take the road and cut in, we'll go slow on the steps."

By the time our shoes sink into the sand, the night sky has cleared. It's one of those natural miracles, and you think that after all someone or something is keeping an eye on you, perhaps wants to see you more clearly. I was glad for Esa because Kate bought him the telescope while she was at a conference in Kuala Lumpur. She kept it hidden for a month at my place before giving it to him for his thirtieth birthday.

We decide on a place close enough to the water so we can hear the waves, but won't be in the path of the tide. The sand is giving after a day of people on the beach. In the back, where the vegetation creeps onto the sand and coral, a family sells Coke, 333 beer, and rents out day huts—similar to beach umbrellas back home, but these are grass roof jobs and set up permanently in the sand. They look closed up for the night.

"Did anyone remember paper?" Kate says.

I tell her I've got some, but I'll need to borrow her lighter in a minute. Esa lets me take charge of the bonfire which is a relief—it gives me something to concentrate on. Even the inside sheets of the newspaper are limp from this weather, but I start with those. I've got the best chance of it not smoking with them. Maggie wandered about under nearby palms looking for twigs, pinecones, anything and she came back with a few twigs, pine, I believe, spiky and thin. (But who knows in a different country what is what? —trees may look the same, the bark, the leaf patterns, the height of the trunk, and then it turns out to be a completely different species. Not related in any way to the one you know in the States.)

Sometimes a fire can take a long time to start. Plays hard to get. Won't submit to the match. I'd already decided on a log-cabin arrangement, but while I pick over the wood on the sand, I think, why be cautious? Why build a box? Let's go for a raging teepee. A burst of flames, hot, thick.

In my opinion, you can't rush a fire. Need to watch it though, that's key. I don't blow too much into it because I can't stay planted here all evening maintaining the glow by my breath alone. So I don't light it up that way. Once it catches, I'll let it build up high. Since we're alone and can rustle up more wood if we need to, I don't see the point of methodical feeding. I need the luxury of excess.

Good, it's taking.

I used to lead kids on canoe trips, and this junior counsellor I had one time seriously wondered whether I was a closet arsonist, said I never looked so content as when I was playing with fire. I seem to be drawn to build and destroy tasks. Cooking is another one.

I take a sip of the beer which was placed next to me in the sand. "I don't know how you can eat those things," I say to Kate, referring to her package of shrimp crackers, and I pass back her lighter. She sucks the salt from her fingertips in lieu of a reply.

I didn't know Tanya well. Should have made more effort, I guess. I think perhaps Maggie knew her in Australia, from Perth both of them? Not sure. But she was young, I had at least ten years on her. When you're only an acquaintance there is less you can do. In an odd way you feel more of a voyeur, a certain guilt gnaws at you. Not so much at what you did to her or said to her one thoughtless day in the corridor at school, but there's an unexplainable desire to be blown apart because her life deserves that much. Surely. Surely a moment of devastation should translate into more than this calm beach scene.

Esa is unzipping his telescope case preparing to set it up. I've built the fire, I've tried to hold up this centre, this piece of sun down here in the sand which we can stare into and not burn out our eyes. It won't fix anything, it isn't a bridge, but it's a physical concrete thing I can do. I'm not good at that other stuff, women's talk. Not my bag. I've got some Scotch though. Will offer some in a minute.

I think the hardest part is I wish my thoughts were nobler. I want to run my fingers through Maggie's hair. Just once.

There it is, there it flies the fire of my youth. You'd think I could concentrate on being something of a pillar for people, her grieving friends. It's the comfort of another body. I don't know. An insistent part of me says I should have been able to prevent what happened—an impossible feat, I wasn't even there. It eats at me nonetheless. Almost as if Tanya were a younger sister. A relative. An uncle. Like my dad's eldest brother who left the farm for Vietnam and returned in a wheelchair. I've never known him with legs. Can't imagine him tossing his daughter's dirt bike into the back of a pickup and giving her a lift home. That's as surreal and inconceivable as what happened this morning.


KATE

On the boat Esa suggested a fire. Or was it Denis? Now I
can't remember. It was a relief to hold onto an anchor, a
plan for later in the day when we would gather and consider. The colourful wooden boat had a dragon's head
carved into the prow—thick yellow paint and a red tongue
bursting through the teeth. I could tell there'd once been a
blue decorative strip like a ribbon near the dragon's antlers.
I know about the undercoat because I sat up at the front for
part of the afternoon as we motored around Ha Long Bay.

I wish I could remember whether I noticed the chipped
paint before or after we found out. Logic insists I contemplated it hours before. Yet looking back there's no way to
separate my memories of her from her fate. Her death is
like a fine net encapsulating her entire existence. You have
to peer through it.

Tanya didn't arrive at the Green Bamboo Café for our
tour van as expected. We were almost late ourselves. Up so
early, and I made Esa and myself some coffee, the grounds
richer than chocolate. And like during the week before
school, I left the coffee on the one electrical burner turned
on low. We made a mad dash, throwing into our day packs
a change of underwear and those silk sleep sacks assuming
(correctly) that the hotel wouldn't have sheets.

That's how it started. A day of bad memory.

While we sped downtown beside the railway tracks on Le
Duan Road, Esa cried out, "What?"

It was as if he was reading my mind, but we haven't
lived together long enough for such a forge to have developed.

"You pressed your thighs against me," he said. "What's
the matter?"

I leaned forward, closer to his ear. When I mentioned the
glass carafe on the stove, he wasn't sure it was off either so
we had to turn back. Good thing we did.

43

By the time we turned up at the café, I knew we hadn't missed the tour because the hawker girls were still at the van windows. How could we know about Tanya? It must have happened before the van pulled away from the curb and before the girls folded the beige sackcloths over the loaves in their baskets.

I hope I remembered to throw in that second pack of Marlboro Lights. This bag is too big. I don't need half of what is in here: business cards, two maps of Hanoi, a pencil sharpener (good grief), empty film canisters. Here it is. Okay, good. No-one else here smokes, well, Maggie does once in a while, but I assume she'll ask if she happens to be in the mood.

While we toured the magical coast, neared Cat Ba Island, the tour guide pointed out shapes to me in the rocks and cliffs. Islands which resembled a rooster or a dragon's back, a dog fighting. This French couple, who I'd only met this afternoon, said it was the most beautiful coastline they'd ever seen.

I think the mist setting the granite to a contrast added to the wonder. For some of the ride, I sat with the figurehead dragon on my right, my bare legs swinging over the side, and when I was too hot there, I sat under the awning. I put my hat on the table which had flowered linoleum tacked down for a tablecloth, and I read *Orlando*. Imagine the mood of this coast thirty years ago. Twenty. There was one cove we passed where I saw metal containers, huge, orange, bruised blue and rusted cream floating in the sea. There was also a clunky streaked liner loaded down with goods. A part of me expected police boats to roar into the bay and arrest smugglers for this stash. The tour guide's son explained it was a Russian ship. Russian cargo. They store the material here. Looked abandoned to me.

The son speaks better English than his father, but is shyer.

Esa thinks the father simply invited him because there was extra room on the boat. They ate the same seafood lunch we did, I noticed, but carry a different travel guide-book—one I've never seen before—while my friends and the tourists on this trip clutch *The Lonely Planet*.

I think there is something wrong with my brain or it's a lack of minerals or a certain vitamin deficiency because I've had trouble recently remembering things. I'm not saying these are earthshaking facts which slip my mind, but to access the past feels such an effort. It feels absurdly difficult. I learned the names, even the Korean names, of all the children in my science classes and then, about a week ago, I looked at the written out names on the class list and I couldn't, for the life of me, bring a picture to my mind of who was who.

I know these kids.

Into April and arbitrarily the connection is cut. The spelling of some names like Min Yung and Yoon Min—pure memory work—well, the bottom fell out.

Esa kissed Tanya on the forehead once. I forget exactly what precipitated it, but I distinctly remember thinking it wasn't necessary. Not hello, not goodbye, some other moment, her straw hat pulled low, with those burnt gold sunflowers around the rim, and with her sharp blue eyes and blond hair, she could have been Finnish too. Anyway, at a barbecue at Denis's parent's house, she showed me the indent the sun hat made on her forehead. Periodically, she'd poke her finger under the band, rub at the tightness of it. Well, Esa happened to come over at one of those moments and he lifted up the brim and kissed her on the dented, red line as if it were a surgical cut, a scar, a slow heal. It was an exaggerated kiss, almost clownish, not sneaky or with a weight to it suggesting a memory of other times, but it startled me.

I tried hard to hide it. I didn't want to appear juvenile or rabid. But that is something I remember. It is clear. The moment he bent down, the moment his lips lifted off her skin, and the start of me trying to be cool about it.

I bet you she was wearing her hat this morning. I bet her hair was still damp from her shower and she'd thrown her red embroidered bag into the front basket of her bicycle. Like me when I cycle, she would loop the straps of her bag over her handlebars to safe-guard against theft or the bag bouncing out from a bump or massive hole in an alley.

It's impossible to believe. I know it happens—all over the world—every day traffic accidents and especially here in Vietnam, officially there's seventeen deaths a day on the roads. The government paper says traffic deaths have quadrupled in the last six months. You wonder how many don't even make it into the papers.

The one absolute I can accept is Denis' fire—the click and crunch of wood devoured by flames and embers. And, in direct contrast, the smooth reach of waves on the beach. That irregular but soothing lapping. Both of these, and then Esa unscrewing the legs of his small but adequate telescope. It was a bother to bring it for a one-night holiday, but I'm relieved he did now. To show Denis and Maggie and me, too, what is out there tonight.

A question of Maggie's: "Let's say you were stranded on a desert island. You could choose one book to have with you. What would it be?" An old party question, the opener, but in a way for us it's necessary. It's as if there is a language barrier in the way of us discussing any part of Tanya, even though she is the reason the four of us are here on this beach drinking adequate copies of name-brand liquor, whatever we could drum up in this town. I don't notice a big difference in real red-label Scotch and the pirated version. The trade has gone on for so long, the method perfected of copying labels, bottle shapes, seals that it is pointless to believe you can spot the, if any, fault. Your only hope, a Viet Kieu man told me, is to develop a rapport with a reputable shopkeeper and ask him to guarantee his liquor, Johnnie Walker say, by autographing the label. But a Vietnamese would never do this for a foreigner he insisted, so I can't understand why he bothered to pass on this unusable information. To show how well he has straddled East and West?

No-one has answered Maggie's question yet. Denis will, I think. Denis will feel obliged to try. But each of us is already alone, and the question should really be: What book do you wish was in your lap right now? New or old favourite.

"I'm not a big reader," Denis says, poking at the fire with a stick.

"How long would you be on the island?" I ask. Half-serious, but mainly stalling.

"You don't know. But you're definitely stranded."

"A book on plants. Edible and inedible ones," Denis says, proudly. He knows this is a good answer. A survivor's answer.

I brush the sticky sand off the tops of my feet, but then burrow them under deeper. They're getting hot from the fire. It is already warm in April here. Not violent heat, but it will come. Soon.

"I guess I'd bring Shakespeare," I say, knowing the Bible is longer. But tomorrow I may say Faulkner or Woolf.... Choosing between all the books I've read would be agonizing. Like knowing when you were going to die, picking the day.

I want to memorize tonight. The four of us sharing Tanya and admitting our shock and perhaps guilt for living by not forcing the conversation. Anything and everything feels permissible. Perhaps that's what death gives: an open field with your perspective not necessarily better, but completely bombed out. You are catapulted out of a manageable decision-making system: order new lab equipment from this catalogue or that one, read this week's mail after my bath or maybe during it. Always placing activities and needs along this chain, string of time, yet now, when you'd think I'd be finally clear on what matters, I can only stand on the lip of this sudden hole in our lives and stare down.

"Can I see?" Maggie says.

Esa peers into the telescope for a few more seconds and then stands straight.


ESA

"If you don't touch anything, it's set on Jupiter. There's a moon—" I watch Maggie wink and peer into the telescope "—crossing the front of the planet."

47

She blinks casually, then her neck goes rigid. "Yeah," she coos. "I see it. That's amazing." And then, "Wowie!"

Face up to the night sky, I'm embarrassed as if I've painted the display myself. I want other people to get excited like I do, but not insincerely. Her brassiness is hard to read, especially coupled with that toothy grin.

Maggie was sipping her espresso-like Vietnamese coffee out of a glass when Kate and I arrived at the Green Bamboo Café. I dashed in and saw her fiddling with the metal filter set on the pilling tablecloth. It was her idea to call Tanya and see if she was still coming. Gregory is out of the country, and we tend to look out for people. Besides, I like Gregory. We play darts at the Cactus sometimes. I still haven't managed to get him into the sauna. A group of us from the embassy go to the ASEAN Hotel on Fridays and take a dry sauna together. He said once, he fancied going, but he wondered if we're a bunch of poofters. Crowd of naked men sweating in a room.

That's a Brit for you.

Maggie had Tanya's phone number so she called, and there were a lot of rings. (I was hesitant calling, considering the time of day, on Saturday too, she might have changed her mind about joining us, but looking back, well, I guess in the scheme of things it made no difference.) Finally a roommate answered, then another long wait, while I glanced out the café window; Kate gesturing that one of the vans was about to leave. Yes, Tanya was gone. Her bicycle not out in the front hallway.

We manoeuvred through the crush of hawkers and piled onto one of the vans. Maggie sat in the folding seat near the window and we, Kate and I, slid into the back one intending to sleep. We were told there were two vans leaving and figured—Denis offered to wait—she'd catch the second one with him, and we'd meet up at the ferry dock in Haiphong about two hours away.

They don't need me at the telescope, and I'd rather sit on one of the rocks someone, probably Denis, dropped near the coals. I want to think about other things, and at the same time, I want to be there. Here. I wish Gregory were with us so I could at least put an arm around him. Jesus.

"How would you explain to a class what the moon's made of?" Denis says. He has taken over the eyepiece.

I shrug. "Old rock."

The cicadas churn in the scrub. I'm amazed there aren't mosquitoes, and I expect it's the fire which keeps them at bay. And Kate's cigarettes.

I imagine on Jupiter's moons, at least on one of them, there'd be ice. A thick ice. And silence. No vegetation or animals, but it wouldn't be lonely, it would be paralyzed, a protective, petrified still. And the only way life would begin would be by it arriving via meteorites or spaceships. Travellers.

It is barren. Moons are. They revolve predictably: they turn and spin and follow through the motions with an instinct for the familiar. This is like my birthplace, Finland, and the people there: my parents; my sister, Marja; some friends. I grew up in Thailand, wild Bangkok, then moved to Japan. At the end of high school, my parents returned with us to Helsinki and their marriage cracked up, shattered within a year. I could have told them this would happen. You can't return to a walled, ice-capped city and expect your body to freeze, in turn, without a fight. My blaze was too strong. All through university, I planned to exit the first chance I could.

In some ways, it doesn't feel as if I left of my own free will. I was ejected, not physically, no policeman seized me by the elbow and steered me to an airplane. It was the rigidity of my parents' land. The landscape invigorates the blood and limbs of millions of Finns, I know this, but it held me by the throat.

Kate's cigarette flies into the dying fire. She's meticulous about them. Whenever we motor out into the countryside, head out to Pottery Village to build up our dish collection, she will grind the Marlboro Light butt into the red dirt, but not leave it, she squats and peels it off the ground, and either cups it or drops it in her pocket. I suppose if she wasn't careful she could set fire to herself. I never thought about it before.

In truth, I like how unwilling she is to corrupt the country. But I think it is a naïve gesture. I think this doi moi will do the job. All these firms shaking with the Vietnamese and starting up joint ventures. These businesses, and the blood clots they create, will sully the countryside. Hell, there are rumors of Club Med in Ha Long Bay, or is it Nha Trang? I want to see as much as I can before the cancer of capitalism sets in.

And I want Kate to quit. So worried and thoughtful about Cat Ba National Park and here she could be corroding from the inside.

A man is making a steady trek across the sand toward us. Maggie has noticed him too—unusual for a male to be selling food—and I'm not particularly concerned because we've been quiet, and it is a public beach. Denis is the one who gets rowdy with drink. He is not an affable drunk, a more abrasive tough guy emerges who demands a lot of attention.

Now I can see he is younger than I first thought, and he's carrying a basket of pineapple, some peeled, the knots carved out in swirling rows about the fruit. Each peeled one is wrapped in a clear bag with a rubber band around the top. While I take this in, a heartburning sigh erupts inside me—it is not a good night for the hard sell. I don't feel generous. "Do you want some?" I say to Kate.

She thinks about this for a moment, lifts her chin as she exhales. "Why not?" she says.

I buy two, accepting the first price he asks. He lingers on the outside of the circle near Denis, and I know if I was a better person I would talk to him, let him practice his English on me, but I just need a break from the same tedious questions. The teenager approaches, sits on his heels behind me, and I feel myself bristle.

"Where you from?" he says in pretty good English.

I pause, hate this question from anyone. I give my standard answer, Finland. Phan Lan.

Most don't know where this is.

It doesn't matter.

Before he can ask another curious question, I say, "Today—Hom ngay." He nods. "My friend, our—" I include everyone with a wave of my hand, they are all watching me now "—chung toi—our friend died." My Vietnamese is very poor and I can see he doesn't understand. "Die," I repeat. All I can think of for telling motions is hands praying and head resting on top feigning sleep, or a finger whisked across my neck as if Tanya's throat was slashed.

Kate's eyes drop to the coals. Denis claps, then flings his hands apart. The teenager glances toward the sound.

"Xe dap—bicycle of my friend," I smack my hands, "with xe om va em ay...." I shake my head. In a last ditch effort, I place my hand over my heart, beat my chest rhythmically and then suddenly stop. It feels important to pass it on. Essential. He raises his eyebrows, and I guess my seriousness and intensity for a young man unnerves him because a weird smile crosses his face before he looks down.

I know it is an intimacy I've shared, and he was not expecting it, but I really don't need this goofy reaction. It's as if he is laughing at our pain. I feel foolish I tried to explain.

Denis says, "Get lost." He picks up a stone.

"He doesn't understand," Maggie says.

Denis tosses it in his hand as you would a set of keys. "Course he does," he mutters.

"Anyone for a swim?" says Maggie.

"Go away," Denis barks, this part in Vietnamese. "We're not fucking entertainment."

I consider that if we make to go swimming, he'll leave. But something else appears to have worked because he abruptly picks up his basket and sets off back across the beach. I watch him now, follow his bare feet in the sand. He knows this is his beach. His family's house. Their bay.

He must think we're lost.

The rift between him and us is not caused by a failure of language. It is not even an echo of wars, it is the fundamental fact that he stays and I go. My home is not butted up against a limestone cliffside, the fired tile roof laid down, the shutters fastened during the monsoon season; I take my home on my back, in my mouth. I'm like a reindeer weaving through fir trees, knee-deep in snow, but I keep on tracking. Sometimes, especially now with Kate, I dare to believe I've found my people.


MAGGIE

I'm sure it's safe. Only small fish would be hugging the shore at this hour. In Australia, you have to worry about jellyfish and sharks. Sharks are everywhere. I asked my driver about them once while I was waiting for Saul to come out of a meeting, and the driver, Minh, said no. Not in Vietnam. I think he'd know if anyone would. I don't intend to wade out past my waist, just frolic near the shore.

"Didn't bring my swim-shorts," Esa says, pulling himself back somehow without actually moving. "Or I would."

I laugh. "Don't believe him for a minute," I say to Kate. "Cheep cheep. Cheep cheep cheep."

"That's it," Denis says. "You two go in, we'll go in."

The problem with dares is that I always want to do them. I feel compelled.

Finally Kate answers, "I think I'd rather drink." She looks at me apologetically. "Be a lump."

I'm a little disappointed, but not a lot. I'm ready to go back to the hotel soon, achy from sitting cross-legged on the sand. In truth, it's more shells and pebbles. Not like where I'm from. At least not the beach nearest to my home. Our home. Tanya was from there too. People at the school seem to think we were good mates. Not really. I mean, we went to the same schools, but she wasn't a close friend. And I expect because she was—let's see—yeah, two years, at least two years below me, I paid even less attention. You know how you tend to notice the older ones, look up to them, study them. I wonder what Tanya thought of me. She probably didn't pay much attention either seeing as she was a brain. Won a scholarship to Queens, I think.

It's such a pity. Such a waste. Poor girl. When I rang her house from the government hotel here—I was supposed to share a front room with her—I got a woman who sounded raw and clipped. She thought I was Gregory, Tanya's boyfriend. You feel so helpless and, even now, a shiver runs down my back. Of course I said if there was anything we could do and that, already considering what the school might do in her honour. Then the tail end of the story spilled out. How Tanya was pronounced dead at the scene, no point in flying her out to Bangkok. Couldn't have been very many people on the road just before six, I think it was. Some Vietnamese surrounded him, the motorbike driver, and made sure he didn't take off. Someone even yanked his keys out of the ignition. No way was I going to ask whether Tanya wore a helmet. Don't think she does. Did, I mean. Most don't on their push-bikes. If you inquire, and it turns out they didn't, it sounds as if you're suggesting the person deserved what happened.

I feel sorry for the driver. He must be terrified.

Thinking about it doesn't help.

Tanya played netball with me a couple of times, and we talked about going tomorrow—some women book the basketball court every Sunday. I didn't think we'd have a hope of getting back in time. Not with a tour of more caves, then there'd be the van ride back to the Green Bamboo. I couldn't take any snaps on the boat today. It felt wrong. Was gorgeous scenery though, those incredible islands, thousands of them with lips of pristine beach. Virgin territory, that's how it felt.

I picked her up in the car once, and we went to the game together. She was anxious about coming; I was surprised. I remember telling her there was a mix of new and old people. Just good fun. Strange she'd never played back home in school—it's very big in Australia. We were early and so stood near the dusty soccer fields (not fields to speak of, dirt yards) waiting for three o'clock to roll around.

She was getting these phone calls, she said. She and Gregory were out on their push-bikes the day before. One Saturday. Two Vietnamese girls, teenagers, started up a conversation, and it wasn't long before Tanya was wandering beside the Red River with them, these two students of

English, and Gregory was following behind, fending off mischievous boys who appeared out of nowhere. Seems they were trying him out as monkey bars.

Listening to her, I was starting to get worried. I know the area of riverbank they walked along, and it's isolated.

They offered her green apples with salt. She was rapt. Afterwards, they all walked their push-bikes back up the ramp to the road, and Tanya said the girls were so enthusiastic, she couldn't refuse them the school address and also her home phone number. But they kept ringing her, she complained.

"Don't you hate that?" I remember saying. "You give somebody your phone number, and then they go and use it."

"How was I to know they'd get obsessive about it?" she said. It seems they rang her house—driving her roommates to distraction—four times in the space of an hour.

"They do tend to cling," I said. "A real live westerner all their own."

"I think they're just young," Tanya said.

Those two Vietnamese girls remind me a bit of my sister and me when we were young. The bold, crazy stuff we'd do. I miss her. One loss reminds you of another, and even though she's not dead (that I know of), she may as well be. One false step of mine years ago, and boom! Justice of the heart can be as indifferent as a butcher. I can't undo the past, it's tied up like a boot. The problem is—or maybe it's the good thing—as Saul says to me on those bad days, your life carries on. You learn to live without her, seal over; it inevitably happens. It's only one night away from Saul, but it feels like an eternity when I start contemplating her.

"Should we make a move?" I say, stretching my legs.

Kate curls over her watch, moves her arm closer to the dying fire. "Looks like 12:15," she says. With the tip of her tongue, she licks her top lip, careful to keep her boil dry. Must hurt. I notice her pocketing a chunk of coral or shell before we all stand up and Denis kicks out the embers.

If I thought it would help, I'd tell everyone here I'm pregnant, as a positive thing to hold onto. But I think

54

tonight should belong to Tanya. It's her moment.

I thought we'd share stories about her, but it's like once she's dead you don't feel right. Like cracking jokes behind someone's back—isn't right. Other parties I've been to, we —usually me, I guess—ask questions like: If you could take up a different career, start over, what would you choose? Or what do you think happens when you die; do you believe in the soul? But when the real situation presents itself—some young woman who is not even married yet is taken away— then those questions seem trivial. They sound forced. Don't like the idea of us four splitting up tonight, at least Kate and Esa have each other. They're not speaking, but you don't have to when your buddy is right beside you. There's a gravitational balance. Not a sharp pull.

Denis gives me his hand, helping me get up to the first step of the cliffside, and even though he's had a fair amount to drink and I'm a little wary of him, I don't want to let go. My hand lingers in his. But before a surprised awareness and possible awkwardness sets in between us, I let go. A conscious thing. If he'd held onto me, I wouldn't have minded. But then what? I'd have to let go at some point.

Kate and Esa are lucky. They are tramping in step ahead, the gravel shifts and rolls under their sandals. The popular ones which are black and chunky and ugly.

While we walk alongside the hotel toward the outside staircase, Denis mutters, "I'm such an asshole."

"What? No, you're not. What do you mean?"

"With that guy on the beach."

"Aw, look. I didn't want him around either. He's tougher than that. It's his business—selling to people who don't want to buy."

"Hmm. Sweet dreams," he murmurs, and walks past me to his door.

I wasn't supposed to be alone in this room. It's too big for just me. Two double beds. I could really use a kiss right about now. Or a man singing to me in a foreign language. That'd be nice. You look for a summation. It's the end of the day (actually the beginning of another one), the end of a life, us left behind and I'm at a loss.

I wonder if I need the mosquito net. It's a bother. Then again there's been a recent case of dengue fever. It's the mosquitoes which come out at night you have to worry about. For the baby, more than for me, I'll tuck the netting under the mattress. A cloth shield. Take the night into me breath after breath and I'll get on okay.

# VIVETTE J. KADY

# Return Stroke

One afternoon during a violent thunderstorm, while my grandmother washed dishes beneath the open kitchen window, lightning struck and her hands caught fire. She sprang away from the sink and stood gaping at her blazing hands until Uncle Hank, who had just come into the kitchen, grabbed a dishtowel and smothered the flames. "Oh my," Grandmother said.

I've invented the "Oh my," but she would have said that.

In her frequent retelling of this incident since its occurrence some 35 years ago, Grandmother has said she felt no real pain—just a quick mild burning sensation in the centres of both palms, and then a sort of tingling that spread up her arms and zapped her heart. Well, zapped is my word —she wouldn't say that.

The fire left no outward traces—no weals of scar tissue or scorched discoloured skin—but soon after she was struck by lightning my grandmother found she had developed a special "talent": she was able to dowse. It was as if the lightning had charged atoms in her body and somehow she was in alignment, in harmony, with the electromagnetic fields of this planet. She discovered her ability to divine the day after this incident, when she was clearing the yard of branches blown down by the storm. She picked up a forked branch and it dipped down, suddenly and forcefully, right over the septic tank.

Grandmother stopped dowsing a couple of years ago, but for more than three decades it was as if her heart, her soul, the entire constellation of molecules that form her could shrug loose and pierce the soil; slip through caves and rocks to deposits of metallic ores, or underground streams.

This became the single most important thing about her, more momentous than the births or deaths or anything else that had or would happen in her life: a stroke of lightning had singled her out.

Grandmother lies in a rented hospital bed in Uncle Hank

and his wife Ellie's house. On the bedside table are boxes of chocolates, an alarming assortment of pills and the TV remote. She has no intention of leaving the bed. In the past few months she's lost first a toe, then a foot, and now her leg below the knee, to gangrene. "I am dying," she announced when told of the need for the latest amputation, as casually as she might say, "It's going to rain today." This was not for dramatic effect, or to elicit sympathy or denials —she merely wanted it acknowledged, up front, so we wouldn't have to skirt around it.

A board-like contraption has been rigged up under the covers to prevent the bedclothes from pressing down on the amputated stump. When the bed is cranked up, she uses the board as a table to play solitaire on, or a few hands of rummy when I visit. Her eyesight has become too weak for reading. She likes me to read the newspaper to her, from cover to cover. She wants to hear headlines, letters to the editor, birth and death notices, reports of business mergers. "Oh my," she says of government corruption, and she titters or gasps at scandals, a coy hand covering her mouth. I skip the more disastrous bits—famine, genocide, mayhem— hoping she won't notice. It sounds crazy, but I'm convinced she is abnormally affected by eruptions of violence, evil and tragedy—bad news is dangerous to her.

My grandmother is a rational woman, inclined toward the scientific rather than the metaphysical. She readily submitted to tests that measured changes in skin potential as she moved over subterranean water; she is familiar with studies suggesting possible detector sites in the human body for magnetic fields—the adrenal gland in the kidney region; the pineal gland at the base of the brain; the retinas of the eyes. She draws parallels between the navigational mechanisms of migratory birds and dowsers. She is adamant in her refusal to believe that what happened to her was a miracle—she will not be allied with paintings that wink or shed tears of blood. She has accepted her talent with the same matter-of-fact resignation she would have shown had she been born cross-eyed, or with twelve toes, or if she'd developed Tourette's Syndrome.

I spent a fair amount of time with my grandmother while I was growing up, after my father died and my mother started dating again. I've watched her body react to hidden signals. I've been with her while she stood transformed, her atoms spinning in an irresistible dance with something beneath the surface.

Grandmother observed certain rituals when she dowsed. First she'd wash her hands in hot water, then take a few swigs of whisky-laced tea from the flask she kept with her. She has always suffered from poor circulation—blood moves sluggishly around her rotund body to her extremities—but she dowsed without gloves, even in cold weather, so she could feel the rod against her skin. Her fingers would be raw, numb with cold, yet the centres of her palms tingled as if their contact with the dowsing rod had reignited molecular memories of the lightning bolt. She favoured a y-stick cut from a willow. She'd stride off across fields in her thick cardigan and muddy boots, a woollen tuque pulled down over her ears, brandishing the y-stick like a tilted crucifix and moving as quickly as her short stout legs would allow. "The faster I move," she'd say, "the stronger the reaction."

These strong reactions were taxing—Grandmother has described the sensations as akin to a series of electric shocks sweeping across her body. She'd tremble with the chills; her teeth would chatter; fear would lurch and somersault in her stomach.

"Have another chocolate, go on," she says. "Do you know, even the police used me, to find bodies?"

I nod. "I remember." I was there, for the first body. Well, not exactly *there*, out with her when she found it, but I was there afterwards, when she came home. That was the summer my mother remarried, when I was fourteen.

"Nowadays they've got radar that can scan underground," she says. "I saw it on the television. They used it in the backyard of that horrible man—the one who kidnapped those children and took such dreadful photographs of them. But all they found buried in his garden were old cow bones."

"I wish you wouldn't watch stuff like that," I say.

"Not that I'd be much good anymore—they'd have to drag me around in a wheelchair. Now that would be a sight—imagine me bumping around out there, dangling my foot over scrub and mud. Go on, take another chocolate. Take a few."

Finding the first body was an accident. Grandmother had been hired by a construction company to dowse for hidden service lines on a long-abandoned site near the outskirts of town. As she tramped over some muddy soil beneath a clump of trees, her y-stick twisted so violently the bark ripped off and tore the skin on her hands. When labourers from the construction company dug, they found the battered body of young Shannon Peterson. She'd been missing for three weeks, last seen leaving for softball practice at a park a few blocks from her home.

The gruesome discovery caused my grandmother to feel as if she'd arrived at the end of something; as if she'd slipped through the safety net of the world and was falling headlong, mouth open. This was the dark side of the gift— a startling, almost unknowable sorrow pulsed outward from her heart.

After this she began to move more cautiously over the earth, waiting for another shock or a fissure that might open up and swallow her. She pushed the terror deep inside and held it there. It has congealed into something wobbly and gelatinous—a bright, throbbing clot.

"While you're here, would you mind helping me bathe her?"

Aunt Ellie fills an enamel basin with warm water, and hands me towels and soap.

"She hates this," Aunt Ellie warns. "She's as bashful as a young girl. But better you than Hank."

We roll my grandmother onto her side, remove her

nightgown, and slide a towel under her. She moans, and closes her watery eyes. I try not to look at the remains of her leg, the exposed stump. Aunt Ellie washes her face and neck, soaps her belly, the pink folds between her legs, her empty flapping breasts. We help her to sit upright. "Oh!" she whispers, and her lips contract, bluish, around the sound. I hold her while Aunt Ellie washes her back. Her crimped skin feels cold and loose. Aunt Ellie pats her dry, sprinkles her with powder, and we help her into a clean nightgown.

"You smell nice," I tell her as I comb her hair. She keeps it bobbed short, parted on one side. It's hardly greying, but beginning to thin. Strands of hair fall and coil like dark pencilled arcs on her pillow. Specks of talcum powder and tiny flakes of skin fleck the pale blue sheets.

Ever since the lightning struck, atmospheric changes have affected Grandmother—the altitude and position of the sun; the strength and direction of the wind; the approach of storms. It was fine when she was doing run-of-the-mill dowsing for wells and tree roots, but once she began to look for bodies, her acute sensitivity extended beyond mere weather conditions. Now even distant events affect her. Misery blows through her, and as the television brings news of war, earthquakes, mutilations, her condition worsens.

I discuss this with Uncle Hank and Aunt Ellie. "You ought to install some sort of V-chip in that thing," I tell them. "Look how it's affecting her. She's disintegrating."

They exchange frowns.

Uncle Hank speaks carefully. "Any doctor will tell you—and she'd be the first to agree—there are perfectly reasonable explanations for her condition."

I know. Poor circulation, immobility, ulcerated flesh, putrefaction, amputation. Infection, amputation. And so on. Vision clouded—age-related. The bedridden have feelings of morbidity. These things happen.

But they cannot deny she has developed a highly unusual sensitivity to the world. Images of massacres in Algeria flicker across the TV screen, and my grandmother's limbs ache. Flood victims weep and her head throbs.

"Listen dear," Aunt Ellie says gently, "it's not good for you to be cooped up with an invalid. You're young. You should be out with people your own age."

"Your grandmother loves that TV," Uncle Hank says. "She likes to keep informed. Her mind's still sharp as a tack."

Grim self-sacrifice pinches the corners of Aunt Ellie's mouth. "Don't get me wrong—we love having you visit, but now's the time to be enjoying your life."

"But I'm *happy* to be here," I protest, and leave the rest unsaid—*besides, she won't be around much longer.*

I do have a life beyond my deteriorating grandmother, and my aunt and uncle who've become impatient and exhausted from the demands of nursing her. I spend hours surrounded by—and in various degrees of contact with—strong, lithe, breathtakingly mobile bodies. We engage in tugs-of-war with gravity; we tease the limits of skin, muscle and air.

Alex could have used that in his documentary about me —tugs-of-war with gravity; teasing limits—although he probably would have said it was over-the-top. *Let your choreography speak for itself. Your dancing is so eloquent, you don't need words.*

I lived with Alex for almost two years. He took rolls of footage of me at rehearsals, on tour, in the park, shopping, cooking—Alex and his camera were everywhere. He had enormous energy—he hardly slept. If he wasn't filming or editing, he'd be baking bread, or taking his motorbike apart, or painting the walls, or speeding down the highway, or calling everyone he knew.

The final argument took place after he'd woken me at 3:00 AM to tell me the lighting designer was undermining my work with subliminal messages, and I had to get rid of him. A week earlier it had been one of the musicians.

"It's no good," I said. "I can't do this anymore."

When I came home from rehearsals that evening, I found Alex lying on his back on the futon with a clear plastic bag over his head, held tight around his neck with elastic bands. Beside the futon were a bottle of tequila and an empty pill container. The new Counting Crows was playing—we'd listened to it for the first time late one night that week with the lights out—but six discs were loaded in the magazine of the CD player. At the moment of his death, Alex could have heard the Brahms Violin Concerto, Tom Waits, Big Audio Dynamite, Cecilia Bartoli or Ali Farka Toure.

There was no suicide note, but on the kitchen counter was a photograph he'd taken of me a few months earlier at a sidewalk sale—I'd tried on a pair of outrageous cat's eye sunglasses with fluorescent orange frames. Alex had cropped the photograph and mounted it on a sheet of rose-coloured cardboard. Diagonally across the cardboard he'd written: *last seen enjoying her illusions.*

That happened eight months ago. The aftershocks are unavoidable. All it takes is the scent of a particular shaving soap, or an inadvertent envelope addressed to the dead, shoved through the mail-slot with bills and flyers and a card from Mother, or some music first heard late with the lights out, and the ground threatens to break open.

In her dreams, my grandmother is falling. She jerks as she sleeps; little spasms shake her like jolts of electricity.

There is something about me that Grandmother and Uncle Hank and Aunt Ellie wouldn't want to know, although it's actually quite harmless, and perfectly safe. For the past few months I've been supplementing my income with phone sex. I have the perfect voice, and it's easy, once you get the hang of it. You can chop celery or sort laundry or do some basic stretches while they're jerking off on the other end of the line. You just have to remember to talk dirty from time to time—it's not hard to figure out what they want—and to keep moaning and breathing heavily. Most of my clients are repeats. Some want to meet me, but of course that's out of the question.

A man is setting up a telescope on the sidewalk diagonally opposite Uncle Hank and Aunt Ellie's house. It's an unusually cold night for the beginning of spring.

Grandmother watches news of oil spills, refugees, nuclear leaks, bombings. A female torso with surgically severed limbs stuffed in a bag near a railway line. Cult suicides, comet madness.

I turn off the TV. "Come outside with me. I want you to see the comet."

"I can't, dear," she says.

"It's perfect tonight—no clouds. There's a guy out there with a telescope. Come."

Uncle Hank helps me lift her into the wheelchair. We put a couple of thick socks on her foot, tuck blankets around her, muffle her with scarf and hat and gloves.

I push her slowly down the front walk and steer her over to the man fiddling with his telescope. He looks quite young. He's wearing a beret and a leather jacket with the collar pulled up over his neck.

"Hi," I say. "Mind if we take a look through your telescope?"

"Sorry. I can't get the comet in focus. My hands are shaking too much—it's so cold." He speaks with an accent I can't place. "It's a delicate instrument."

"What a shame," Grandmother says.

"You can see without the telescope," and he points to it —clear and bright, its tail streaming upwards.

"My grandmother's eyesight's not good," I explain.

"Then we'll have to keep trying." He lowers the stand, crouches down, repositions the angle of the telescope, blows on his hands and rubs them together, makes minute adjustments to the eyepiece. "Okay," he says after a few minutes, "I have it." Little fires of exhilaration dance in his black eyes.

We manoeuvre the wheelchair so that Grandmother can have a look.

"Oh my—how wonderful!" she exclaims.

When I take my turn at the telescope, Grandmother says, "I've heard that every carbon atom inside each one of us comes from some distant star." After a few moments, she adds, "My granddaughter here is a dancer." She is gazing up, apparently transfixed by the vast, spinning night sky.

I laugh. "My grandmother here has a remarkable ability to navigate."

Aunt Ellie brings cups of hot tea after we get Grandmother back to bed.

"Perhaps that young man out there would like some tea to warm him up. I'd like a drop of whisky in mine, Ellie, for a nightcap. It was terribly cold outside."

"That'll be the day—not with all the medication you're taking," Aunt Ellie says. "You should rest when you finish your tea. Be sure you don't overdo it."

"Good heavens, I'll have more than enough rest when I'm dead. If I had both legs, I'd go dancing." After Aunt Ellie has gone, she sighs and pats my hand. "A daughter-in-law is not the same as a daughter."

"Your hands feel warm tonight," I say. There are small clusters of blister-like eruptions in the centres of both palms. "How long have you had this rash?"

"I hadn't noticed. It must be a reaction to all these pills." She sips her tea and pulls a face. "Want to play a few hands of rummy before you go?"

I shuffle the cards.

"Remember how my hands caught fire, in a lightning storm?" she says. "Well, of course you couldn't *remember*, you weren't born yet. You know, lightning isn't just one single stroke that falls to earth and then that's over and done with. There's some give-and-take involved."

I begin to deal the cards. "What do you mean?"

"Well, apparently the thundercloud sends down negative charges, but before they reach the ground, opposite charges from houses or trees—or my soapy hands, for that matter—rush to meet them somewhere up there. You see, there's mutual attraction." She picks up her cards, sorts them. "All that energy and fury—the flash of light, the thunder—is really from what they call the return stroke, which goes back up to the cloud. It moves so quickly, we can't see it's actually rising, not falling." She picks up a card from the top of the pack and smiles.

I lower her bed, smooth the sheets, kiss her forehead. "So," Grandmother says, and blinks. Her eyes say the rest—*I am dying. Have another chocolate. Take two. Go on.*

When I close my eyes she is there, an after-image on the retinas.

My grandmother taught me never to bathe or use electric appliances during a thunderstorm. I will hang up the phone when there's lightning, even if my client is in the final throes of passion. If I'm caught outside in an electrical storm, I know not to shelter under a tree. I'll look for the lowest point and crouch, keeping both feet on the ground.

# Detour

The month after he got out of rehab, Frank made a 110-mile detour on his way to his brother's wedding. He first drove an hour south to see the Francis Bacon exhibition, then headed north-east so he could pick up the interstate. He hadn't planned this beforehand. He'd already been driving for about fifteen minutes when he remembered that the exhibition—Bacon's Popes—would be closing soon, so he took the first exit and looped south.

He stood in the gallery, surrounded by screaming popes, and what struck him most was the lack of violence in the paint application. He'd expected fierce, explosive brushstrokes, but from up close the paintings were very controlled, almost subdued.

When he got back into his car, he thought that he should probably find a phone and call to let Rob, his brother, know he'd be late, but he decided not to bother. The wedding wasn't until the following afternoon. He pushed an old Ry Cooder cassette into the tape deck, and as he drove he thought about what he would tell Rain, the woman his brother was marrying, about the Bacon exhibition. *Masterful technique*, he would say. *Stand right in front of a painting and you can't make it out, it's just colours. But move back six feet and the eyes jump out at you.*

Ry Cooder was singing, "Little sister won't you please, please, please...."

*The popes look as if their bones are dissolving*, he would say. *They're raising fists, or cowering, or shouting dogma. But they're blurred, pulpy, evaporating.*

Frank drummed the steering-wheel and sang along, "Little sister don't you kiss me once or twice, say it's very nice and then you ru-u-un, woo woo woo woo...."

*Most days I feel like those popes*, he would say. *Like I could just open my mouth and howl.*

He tried to conjure up Rain's face, but all he came up with was the image of a lockjawed pope. Rob and Rain. Christ, the alliteration should've been enough to get them to call off the wedding.

He turned up the volume on the tape deck and rolled down the window. He liked driving. He'd be happy to go on doing it, day after day, criss-crossing the continent and watching the miles unravel. Washing in gas-station restrooms; drinking coffee from styrofoam cups; pulling over on back roads and reclining the seat when he needed sleep. He liked the shift in perspective that came with speed: the funnelled pull of the road; that swift freefall through landscape until he became the stationary point, the still centre, while trees and buildings and signs hurtled past.

Going to this wedding was Frank's biggest test since rehab. It was one of the hardest things he'd ever had to do. Maybe he and Rob would pummel one another in the middle of the ceremony with that fierce, murderous fury particular to brothers. "Are you okay with this?" Rob had asked when he called to say he was getting married, and Frank knew that whatever answer he gave, it wouldn't make a bit of difference. That's how it was with Rain.

*You know how you look at something and suddenly it all makes sense*, he could tell her. *It's like God comes down for a moment.*

And then she'd smile that crooked, wicked, moist-lipped grin that made his knees collapse.

*I'm still crazy in love with you*, he could say. *Marry me instead.*

A half-hour from his brother's place, Frank broke into a sweat. No telling what he might do, but he was pretty sure it was going to be something stupid. He pulled over at a gas station, filled the tank and bought a Coke, a pack of Marlboros and some gum. In the men's room, he splashed water over his face and hair, changed his t-shirt, and realized he was definitely planning to win Rain back.

He hadn't seen her for twenty years, but he'd never stopped loving her. Not even while he was married. Anna, his wife, left him the night (or early morning, technically) he smashed the Honda into a parked car a few blocks from their house. The cops had found him walking down the road, totally naked but unhurt, a couple of doors from home. He tried to explain to the police, and later to Anna, that he was naked because there was a hot tub at the party. The party was full of *industry types*, he kept saying. Movie pricks so thick you tripped over them. "*Vanity Fair* wants me to photograph Tarantino," he told them, but nobody cared.

"You just *consume* everything," Anna had said when he tried to stop her from leaving. "Whatever it is, you'll keep on and on until it's all used up. Drugs, booze, love, everything."

That was six months ago, but it had been a long time coming.


Rain was an art student named Sharon Riley when Frank fell in love with her. Sharon reinvented herself as Rain—legally, with new ID—back when people were still naming themselves or their children after celestial bodies, or seasons, or various expanses of water.

"Why *rain?*" Frank had asked, running a finger down her beautiful spine. "Rain's such a bummer. It's cold and wet and nasty."

"No, not *that* kind," she'd said, her voice muffled by the pillow. "The gentle kind. Soft and misty."

"Ah," he said. "Drizzle."

They spent two years together, then she left him for a diamond cutter. The day she packed her bags, they sat on the bed for a while. Whenever he tried to say something, she shook her head and brushed her fingers over his mouth. "I'm not changing my mind," she said.

And now he couldn't even picture her face. Every time he closed his eyes, all he could see was a screaming pope.


It was evening when Frank pulled up outside his brother's house. He figured the Escort parked in the driveway had to belong to his mother—the vanity plates read *BI Z B*. He turned off the ignition, leaned back and shut his eyes. He stayed like that for ten or maybe twenty minutes, every vein in his body pulsing, until there was a rap on the side of the car.

"Frank?" Rob's smile was uncertain, as if he thought Frank might be someone else.

"Shit," Frank said. "You gave me a heart attack."

"You okay? We were getting a little concerned."

"I'm fine. Took a bit of a detour."

"You just sitting here?"

"I was about to come in." Frank got out of the car and pointed at the Escort. "Mom's here?"

"Uh-huh. In full force."

"Running around like a blue-assed fly?"

"Absolutely."

Frank shook his head. "Busy bee? Shit. What the hell was she thinking?"

Rob grinned and slapped an arm around Frank's back. "Hey. It's good to see you."

"Likewise."

He squeezed Frank's shoulder. "It means a lot to us. Really."

Frank removed his bag, his camera equipment and the wedding present from the trunk. He'd bought a large, asymmetrical copper vase, and immediately regretted the purchase. It cost too much and looked as if it had been flung against a wall numerous times. The woman in the store had gift-wrapped it really nicely, though. She'd sprinkled a handful of small silver stars inside the box, and then she'd curled thin strands of pale green and black ribbon around it. He wasn't going to return the vase once she'd gone to so much trouble.

"Here," Frank handed Rob the gift. "This is for you." He lit a Marlboro. His hands were trembling. "Where's Rain?"

"Gone to pick up the flowers. She'll be back soon. Please don't smoke inside, okay?"

Frank exhaled slowly. "Okay." He took a few more drags on the Marlboro, then flicked it under a shrub. His brother had a nice garden, and a nice house in a secluded neighbourhood. He was a partner in a law office.

"Mom?" Rob called as he ushered Frank indoors. "Look who I found."

Their mother appeared at the kitchen door. "Oh Frank."

71

She wiped soapy hands on her apron. She was huffing from all the running around. "You made it."

"Hi Mom," Frank said, and kissed her. She was plump and soft and she smelled like an odd mixture of vanilla and onions.

"We were worried." She flapped her hand in front of her nose and frowned. "You're smoking again?"

Frank shrugged. "One thing at a time."

"Cut him some slack, Mom," Rob said. "He just got here."

"We expected you hours ago," she said.

"I was delayed. Nice car."

She looked confused.

"The Escort? Outside?" Frank said.

"Is that how long since you were here? That's the car Rob bought me. Isn't it wonderful?"

"Gorgeous," Frank said. He desperately needed to put something into his mouth. "Got any coffee?"

"I'll make some," Rob said. He patted Frank's stomach, which was newly toned after weeks of obsessive post-rehab sit-ups. "You're looking good. Doesn't he look good? There's a towel in the bathroom if you want to take a shower or anything."

Frank sniffed under his arms. "I'm okay."

"Now Frank," their mother lowered her voice and gave him a worried look when Rob went into the kitchen. "You're not going to cause any trouble, are you?"

He felt the heat spread over his face. "Come on, give me some credit."

She sighed. "Because it's going to be such a nice wedding. Everything's running smoothly."

"That's good," he said.

"Although I wonder if Rob has any idea what he's getting into." Her mouth tightened. "That girl is *not* easy."

"Rain?"

"Oh, Rain's no angel. But that daughter of hers is impossible."

She might as well have swatted Frank right off his feet. His breath caught in his throat. "She has a daughter?"

"You didn't know? Two children. A girl and a boy."

Frank felt suddenly old, and sadder than he'd been in years. Until this moment, he'd somehow believed that Rain would still be the same as she was the day he last saw her.

"She stole her mother's car this morning. Right in the middle of everything, she decides to go on a little joyride. That girl needs a good whack on the you-know-what." She cleared her throat and muttered, "Speak of the devil."

Frank turned around. A kid clomped toward him in killer platform shoes. She looked nine or ten at the most, but her bleached hair was cropped short to reveal multiple ear piercings, and she was wearing a couple of flimsy tank tops and a slinky skirt that had a thigh-high slit on one side. Her eyes were rimmed with glittery blue, her lips were glossed silver, and she was scowling.

"Molly," his mother said, "this is Frank. My other son."

"Wow." Frank blinked. He didn't know whether to pat her head or shake her hand. "Molly? Well. Hi there." He wondered how a kid that small could see over the steering-wheel. And even with those monster platforms, how could she reach the pedals?

She hooked her thumbs in the waistband of her skirt, thrust her hips forward and stared at him. "I'm not a little kid, I'm fourteen," she announced in a bored, flat voice. "I'm small for my age."

"Oh," he said. He was smiling and frowning at the same time. "So. You're Rain's daughter." He tried to figure out which parts of her looked like Rain. Something about the eyes. And the chin, definitely.

Irritation flickered across her face. She turned to Frank's mother. "When are we gonna eat?"

Frank's mother took a deep breath. "Soon," she said. "Aren't you looking after your brother?"

Molly shrugged. "He's watching TV."

"There's plenty to do around here if you're bored, young lady."

Molly rolled her eyes.

"Coffee's ready," Rob called.

"Well, I'll get busy again," his mother said, and headed

back to the kitchen.

Molly opened her mouth wide, stuck out her silver-studded tongue and waggled it at his mother's retreating back. Frank grinned. "So," Molly said, fixing her blue-rimmed gaze on him. "How was rehab?"

"Excuse me?"

Molly glanced sideways and sighed dramatically. "Oh great," she muttered. "The bitch is back." She stomped off, and Frank saw that the front door was open, and Rain had come in.

She was carrying a bucket of flowers. "Ohmygod," she said. "Frank."

"Hey Rain." His jaw shook when he smiled. "You look great," he said, and meant it. Her face had loosened, become softer and sadder, but she was still beautiful.

Rain put down the flowers and hugged him, carefully. Frank's heart slugged and thumped. Then she opened her arms, slid sideways from his grasp and jerked a thumb at the door. "Help me bring in the flowers?"

Frank was having his third after-dinner coffee. He drank it quickly, because he needed another cigarette. "The popes obsessed Bacon for years," he said. "Every time he finished another one, he thought he still hadn't got it right. He said he was trying to perfect the representation of the human cry." He'd rehearsed this earlier, in the car, but the only person who seemed remotely interested was Molly. Her eyebrows rose briefly, then plunged into a frown.

They were folding napkins and making centrepieces. Frank's mother had brought over a Martha Stewart magazine. Cardboard, florist's wire, blue metallic paper and flowers littered the living-room floor. Dash, Rain's son, was supposed to fill bowls with candied almonds, but he kept shoving them in his mouth or dropping them, and those that eventually ended up in the bowls were sticky and covered in carpet fibres. Dash was a tiny, semi-toothless, bulbous-kneed six-year-old with a thin face, dark eyes, and skin like speckled eggshell. Frank thought he didn't look much like a kid at all—he looked like a miniature optometrist from New Jersey.

"There's enough misery in this world," Frank's mother announced. "I don't need to see paintings of it."

"Who is this guy?" Rob asked.

"Francis Bacon?" Rain said. "You know—all those triptychs? He painted mangled torsos. And people who look as if they've been smeared across the canvas by a bus or something."

She sat cross-legged on the floor. She was barefoot and tanned and her dress had thin straps that kept sliding off her shoulders. Frank's jaw clenched and his knee jiggled. He wanted to reach over and hook his finger under a strap.

Rob shook his head. "Nope. Doesn't ring a bell."

"Oh well," she said. "You're not missing much. It's pretty bleak stuff."

"That's not a centrepiece," Frank's mother said, frowning at Molly. Molly ignored her. She was hunched over, bending and twisting wire into what seemed to be stick figures in pornographic poses.

Rain looked up. "Not bad, Molly."

"She's artistically gifted, like her mother," Rob said.

Molly held up two figures intertwined in an impossibly athletic coupling. Her expression was blank. "They're for on top of the wedding cake."

Frank's mother clucked her tongue and muttered to herself.

"Where's cake?" Dash asked.

"Tomorrow," Rob said. "Cake's tomorrow."

Dash tugged at Frank's T-shirt. He'd had enough of the almonds. "Wanna play cards?"

"Maybe. Which game?"

"Go Fish!"

"I don't know that one."

Dash blinked at him, disbelieving, his translucent eyelids veined bluish. "Come," he said with a slow smile, and tugged harder.

"Tell you what," Frank said. "I'll go have a cigarette, then we'll play."

75

Molly looked up from her wire figures. "Watch out," she warned. "He cheats."

Frank sat outside and smoked. He tilted his head back and blew smoke rings, and when he squinted it looked as if they were lassoing stars. In the morning a party supply truck would drive up and offload tables and chairs and a tent, and this place would be transformed. He would help spread starched white tablecloths and carry boxes of booze (*No problem*, he would say to Rob, *I can handle it*) and wipe dusty tumblers. What the hell had he been thinking? That he was so irresistible she'd stop making centrepieces while he swept her off her feet? And then there she was, her bare feet padding so quietly he felt the air move before he heard her.

"How're you doing, Frank?" she said softly.

"I'm okay," he said. "How about you?"

She sat beside him, curved like a comma, her hair falling forward. Her strap had slipped down again. He pushed it back over her shoulder, his fingers lingering for a moment. *Happiness is this close,* he could whisper, rolling the strap between thumb and forefinger.

She straightened her back, shifted her shoulders and smoothed her dress over her knees. "Thanks," she said. "Can I have some of that?" She held out her hand for his cigarette.

He fumbled for the pack. "Here, you want one?"

She shook her head. "I don't smoke anymore." She plucked the cigarette from his fingers, inhaled deeply and coughed. "It's a beautiful night," she said when she'd stopped coughing.

Frank cleared his throat and tried to think of something to say. After a while, he said, "Dash is a funny little guy, isn't he? Kind of—*old*, you know? He doesn't talk a whole lot, but you get the feeling he knows exactly what's going on."

"Dash? He's always been like that. He's a wise old soul."

"Interesting kid. They both are. Molly's a lot like you. Feisty. And smart."

She gave a little laugh that sounded like a hiccup. "She'd

76

be mortified if she heard that. She hates me."

"She's supposed to. She's a teenager."

"Oh, I don't know. She's really angry. She wants to go back to Michigan."

"To *Michigan*? You're kidding. Why?"

She smiled her slow, lopsided grin. "Come on, you've never been there. It's not that bad. She's missing her friends and everything."

"Actually, I have. I once did a photo shoot in Ypsilanti."

"Yeah? It's nice around there."

"It's okay." He lit another cigarette. "So why doesn't she go back and live with her father for a while or something?"

"He's dead."

"Shit," Frank said. "I'm really sorry. I had no idea."

She nodded. "Last September."

"The diamond cutter?"

"The what? Oh, no. God. I'd forgotten about him. No. That didn't last." She looked up at the stars for a while, then she turned to him. "How do you *do* that—the smoke rings? They're perfect."

He passed her the cigarette. "Pretend you're a fish."

"It's like skipping stones. I could never get it right." She inhaled, contracted her lips, puffed out smoke. "See? Useless." After a few moments she said, "He killed himself. Gary, my husband. One afternoon he drove out to this lake where his family always rented a cabin and he drowned himself." Her voice was low and slow.

Frank's mouth was dry. "Could have been an accident."

She shook her head. "No."

When she stood up a couple of minutes later, she said, "Your brother's a good guy, Frank. A really decent, solid guy."

Frank slept at his mother's house that night. He lay in the dark in his old bedroom and thought about the way he'd held Rain in his heart all those years, and how he knew nothing about her. He couldn't remember if she'd always been such a mystery to him. He didn't know anything anymore. He didn't know what happened to love, or how it got used up, or what made people restless, or why they kept hurting themselves. He thought of the way some lives unfolded like long, empty roads, and he wondered what terrible kind of loneliness could make a man gaze out at the deep middle of a familiar lake one afternoon and calculate the weight it would take to sink down and hold himself beneath its skin.

They held the ceremony in the back garden. Frank handed Rob the wedding ring, and stood by as his brother slipped it on Rain's finger, pulled her close and kissed her.

When it was over, Frank took photographs. He took pictures of Rob and Rain, who mugged for the camera, and he took pictures of his mother, who squeezed his arm and told him how pleased she was that everything was turning out so well. He photographed Molly, who was sullen at first, but became animated after she'd downed a few glasses of champagne, and stuck out her tongue for a close-up. He photographed Dash's sweet gap-toothed grin as he crawled out from under a table, and he photographed a couple of bemused guests examining the wedding cake, which was crowned by Molly's wire creation. He took photographs of the buffet table, and later of people jostling in line and pouncing on the food.

He made small talk with distant relatives and acquaintances he hadn't seen in years, and he gave a speech, a toast to the bride and groom, in which he mentioned that he'd known Rain for a long time. He made a crack about how he'd tested the waters for his little brother, and how pleased he was that Rob had obviously inherited his excellent taste. He went on to say what a good guy his brother was, and how fortunate Rob and Rain were to have found one another. His mother dabbed her eyes as she raised her glass, and Frank recalled that Rob had been his best man when he married Anna eight years ago, but Frank didn't remember much of that wedding because he'd been pretty much out of it the whole time. He did recall that at some point he'd unwrapped wedding gifts and attempted to auction them to the assembled guests, who'd howled with laughter as

Anna, shaking her head and grinning, led him away.

He sat beside his mother while they ate, and she cupped her hand over his on top of the table. "I wish you'd visit more often," she said, and Frank looked down at her hand and was shocked to see how she'd suddenly aged.

Rob and Rain had hired an R & B band. Frank sipped a Coke while he listened to them play and watched people dance. The band was surprisingly good. Then Rain grabbed the microphone from the vocalist and belted out something bluesy and sweet. Her hips gyrated and her shoulders swayed and she was mesmerizing. He had no idea she could sing like that. When she finished, everyone cheered and clapped and Rob stood there with a delirious grin on his face, unable to take his eyes off her.

The music was loud and people were shouting and laughing. Everyone looked happy in a jagged, frantic kind of way. Frank chewed the ice at the bottom of his glass and thought of Anna again. Anna used to say she was allergic to parties. Mysterious ailments would surface at the last minute—earaches, toothaches, rashes—so she didn't have to go. The night they first met, at a gallery opening, she'd stood alone, fingering the necklace around her long throat and looking miserable. He'd approached her by asking, "Did somebody die or is it the art?" and her sudden smile was like a door flung wide. "Party catatonia," she'd replied.

It surprised him how much he wanted Anna to be there at that moment. He decided he'd go inside and call her. He'd tell her he was calling in the middle of his brother's wedding reception. He went into the house and found a phone in the master bedroom. He wondered if he had the right number—he couldn't remember when last he'd called. He hoped she wasn't going to cry, or hang up on him. As he dialled the number, he panicked that some guy might answer. After six rings he got her answering machine. Her voice sounded upbeat, encouraging, but he hung up without leaving a message.

Rain cornered him as he came out of the bedroom. She was flushed and her eyes sparkled. "Ah, there you are," she said. "We need to take some pictures of you."

"Forget it," he said. "I hate being photographed."

"Oh, come on," she said, and steered him out of the house. "There are no pictures of you anywhere. Twenty years from now we'll look at the albums and wonder where the hell you were."

She recruited Molly to take the pictures—"She has a great eye," Rain said—and Frank obediently put his arm around Rain, and then his brother, and then his mother, and smiled for the camera.

When Rain was satisfied that Molly had taken enough photographs of him, Frank walked around to the front of the house. He thought that it was almost over; all he needed was to get through that night, and in the morning he would head home. He stood in the street and lit a cigarette. He would try Anna's number again, later on, from his mother's house. And then he thought that there was no need to wait until morning. He could leave right away, drive through the night, and get there before the sun came up. He felt exhilarated. He hadn't been this happy in a long while. He heard the distant laughter and music and felt as if he were already miles away, the long road unfurling in his headlights.

# Soft Spot

Nick sits on Aura when the baby cries at night. He straddles her, all one-eighty-plus pounds of him, pinning down her arms, pressing powerful thighs and feet against her skinny flailing legs. She struggles and swears; she tries to bite him; she squirms and whimpers and aims a knee at his naked balls but he holds firm. The baby howls, and Aura jerks and sobs.

It's only supposed to take a few nights. Forty minutes the first time, then thirty or twenty, and by the fourth or fifth night the baby should get the message. But his wailing gets progressively worse until it's an hour-long frantic juddering, and on the fifth night Aura wriggles and heaves and breaks free.

Later, she dreams she can't find the baby. She wakes and she's crawling around the foam mattress, drowning in the dark, hands fumbling like blind fish toward the ceiling. She dreams this, and wakes like this, over and over.

Most of the time it's dark inside. They're in a basement apartment, and Nick keeps the drapes drawn. He slips in and out, glancing sideways, because as far as the welfare people are concerned, only Aura and the baby live here. Sometimes he goes out and doesn't come back for a couple of days.

Aura opens the drapes when Nick's not around. Watches legs go by. Slides the window wide to smell the weather. When the bellowing from the white house across the street gets too loud, a girl—she's maybe twelve, or thirteen—comes out and plays her trumpet on the porch. The girl stands up there with her eyes closed and her shoulders swaying, and blasts away.

Aura sings to the baby, songs she makes up. She dances while she sings, rocking him in her arms and jiggling him. She's a singer-poet, like Courtney Love, and one day she'll blow them all away.

Nick tells her to shut the fuck up, he's trying to sleep.

They hadn't planned on a baby, but even before Aura was pregnant, she'd skim fingertips over Nick's skin and they'd choose names. Swift. Sahara. Homer, Caius, Silver. This was when they were crashing on Nick's brother's floor. Zen, or Zed. Nick vetoed Zed because of that part in *Pulp Fiction*: "Zed's dead, Baby, Zed's dead." Jak. Jemima. Lily or Lark.

When two blue lines appeared on the test stick from the drugstore pregnancy kit, Aura pictured a beautiful brown-eyed baby girl with an irresistible smile. She'd carry the baby strapped to her back. It would come on tour with the band Aura was going to get together, and she'd bring it onstage, dressed in incredibly cool clothes, like Courtney Love did with Frances Bean. Tiny fur-lined coat, velvet floppy hat, miniature patent-leather shoes.

Aura examined her changing shape in the cracked bathroom mirror. She knotted her T-shirt beneath her swelling breasts and stroked her expanding belly as she swung her hips in slow circles. She grinned at herself and pouted and licked her lips. She slid a hand under the waistband of her panties as she danced to the music in her head, grinding and pushing faster and faster. Then she threw up.

He's not a beautiful baby. His ears jut out and he gets blotchy rashes. His legs dangle, stick-thin and bandy, or tuck up when he shrieks. He's all appetite and voice; a frenzied, beating thing. He frowns as he pulls at her breast, smacking and sucking, a sour-milk smell steaming off him. His head presses into the crook of her arm and she wonders about the things that bind them—buried, silent things encoded in blood and bone.

Aura's hair is growing out. Dark brown roots; pink and yellow at the ends. She walks around the apartment wearing lilac or lime-green or fuchsia slips, lace-edged and stained. They rustle when she moves, kiss her bruised thighs, slide over her belly and breasts. Makeup smudges under her eyes. Open lipstick tubes and magazines and scraps of paper with scribbled song lyrics litter the floor. She smokes cigarettes down to the filters; forages for butts in the ashtrays. She picks up an old issue of *Spin* but there's no time to read because the baby cries. When she goes to him he palps the air with fists and feet.

The towel rail is on the bathroom floor. She went berserk one night, strung out after some bad dope, and ripped it right off the wall.

Nick draws the baby while it sleeps. He draws Aura nursing the baby. He draws his own feet. He's good. He uses anything he can find to draw with—ballpoint pens, chewed eyeliner pencils, lipstick. He draws on envelopes and flyers. Sometimes he does chalk pictures on downtown sidewalks, and passersby give him money. Aura goes with him when she feels like it. She spreads a blanket on the sidewalk alongside him for her and the baby. Nick gets more money when people see the baby.

Aura hates the gloom inside the basement apartment. She scoops up the baby and takes him out for a walk. She carries him until her arms get tired and her feet hurt, then she finds a bench or some steps to sit on and lays him across her lap. When it's grey or windy they go into the conservatory in the park and sit by the waterfall. She shows him orchids and cacti and his eyes are bright river pebbles.

She goes for hours without eating, and sometimes she goes for days without speaking to anyone.

She passes the white house across the street and the girl on the front porch jeers at some boys going by. The girl plays her trumpet while someone shouts inside the house and things crash against walls. The girl doesn't miss a note. When Aura stares too long, the girl stops playing and gives her the finger, *Fuck you.*

She watches the baby jerk or grimace or suck in his sleep. Dreaming of food, or being twisted from her. When she's stoned, she puts him beside her on the foam mattress and stares at the tip of his tongue moving between his lips. Tiny blue veins on translucent eyelids. Bright blood pulsing under new skin. She falls asleep and when she wakes he's screaming and she's forgotten who she is.

Nick brings them presents. A rubber giraffe for the baby. A McDonald's plastic cup. An old toaster oven. Dope.

One afternoon Aura and the baby come back from a walk and there's a TV in the middle of the floor. She asks Nick where it came from and all he says is, "Don't worry about it."

She hates the gloom so she takes the baby and wanders. She walks for hours while he shifts or sleeps in her arms. Sometimes he's so heavy she thinks she'll drop him. He'll slip away, slide from her aching arms.

One rainy day they drift in and out of stores and she shoplifts some powder-blue Hard Candy nail polish. Back in the apartment, she paints the baby's fingernails and toenails and then she paints her own. When she's done, she turns the bottle upside-down to read the name of the colour. "Sky," she tells the baby. "That's a cool name. Maybe we should have called you Sky."

Nick brings them things: a fold-up garden chair; an old stroller; an Asterix book with a torn cover. Nick and Aura read Asterix together on the mattress, giggling, while the baby sleeps on Nick's chest. When the baby wakes, they prop him up so he's sitting between them, and laugh when he topples over. Aura gives him her great-grandmother's silver bracelet to teethe on. They eat peanut butter sandwiches and watch *Jeopardy* and wish they had cable.

Nick brings a stereo, and Aura won't ask where it came from. Then he doesn't show up for a few days and she worries someone will come looking for him. She keeps the drapes drawn and watches *The Young and the Restless* and *Oprah* with the volume turned low, and wishes she could get high.

The night she left home, with a guy who'd once done

time for auto theft, her father said, "I wash my hands of you." Her mother cried. She ran out after Aura, grabbed her wrist and said, "Please." They live a hundred and ten kilometres away and she hasn't seen them for almost four years. They probably think she spends all day shooting up in a dark room.

She watches the news, strumming her guitar and singing softly while houses burn and planes crash, and she wonders if Nick is bleeding or sick or dead.

When he comes back he tells her it's okay, he just had to take care of some stuff.

Aura doesn't buy the conspiracy theory bullshit—Courtney Love had nothing to do with Kurt Cobain's death. Four days after her band released its second album, her husband put a shotgun to his head and pulled the trigger. There was enough smack in his bloodstream to kill him anyway.

Courtney Love called her band Hole because of something her mother told her: *You can't go walking around with a hole in yourself just because you had a bad childhood.*

The baby cries at night and Nick rides her thrusting bucking body and laughs.

One wheel wobbles on the stroller Nick brought, but it's easier than carrying the baby. She pushes him through parks and alleys and under bridges, and doesn't speak for hours. She's suspended high above words; syllables are becoming distant, glinting things. She feels an unexpected lightness, and a word glides by: *joy.*

One afternoon as she pushes the stroller in front of the white house across the street, the girl comes out and slams the screen door. "Suck it up!" she yells over her shoulder. She looks at Aura and Aura waits for the fuck-you finger but the girl says, "Oh look, you've got a baby!" and leaps down the porch steps. She stands grinning in front of the stroller. "I love babies. Boy or girl?"

"Boy," Aura says.

The girl is wearing baggy khaki pants and she's braided

strands of hemp and coloured feathers into her hair. She directs a variety of facial expressions and cooing sounds at the baby. "Hey, he likes me. He's smiling. I'll babysit for you. I'm crazy about babies. If you want a break, like, you know, a night on the town—"

Aura laughs. She finds this unbelievably funny—*a night on the town*. The girl seems bewildered. She looks a bit like Aura's kid sister, who's wanted to be an astronaut since she was eight years old and spends every school holiday at a camp for science geeks. Or maybe she no longer wants to be an astronaut, because she must be sixteen already, and their mother is probably finding bras between the couch cushions and money missing from her purse.

Aura stops laughing. "Sure." She smiles at the girl. "Thanks."

When Aura and the baby get back a couple of hours later, the girl waves from the front porch. "Hey, wait up!" she shouts. She dashes into her house for a moment, then runs across the street carrying some plastic shopping bags. "My mom says you can have these. We don't need them anymore."

Aura looks inside the bags: baby clothes, a crocheted yellow blanket, a purple stuffed elephant, a rattle. She opens her mouth but words slip by, wafer-thin.

The girl takes the rattle from the bag, shakes it, then hands it to the baby. He puts it in his mouth. "I gotta go," she says. "Bye-bye baby."

Aura gives Nick a box of pastels for his birthday. He brings a bottle of tequila and some doughnuts. He's bummed because it's his birthday and all he's managed to score is some hash. She sings Happy Birthday and he blows out the candle she shoved into a chocolate doughnut. He tells her he wishes he'd be discovered by a famous art critic.

"You shouldn't have told," she says. " Now it won't come true."

Nick says maybe they should move someplace warm. Winter's coming, and you can't draw on sidewalks when there's snow. Aura lets the baby suck her chocolatey finger, and says she won't squat freezing warehouses or sleep on park benches or in all-night coffee shops, never again.

Nick tries out his new pastels on the wall behind the mattress. He draws a mural of a beautiful woman leaning out a yellow window, and under the window is a grinning crocodile wearing a suit. The woman has black hair and scarlet lips and she looks bored. Aura worries about the landlord, but Nick tells her to chill, it'll wash off.

They finish the tequila and when she wakes it's daylight and the room blurs and spins. Nick's not there and she's forgetting something. Then she realizes the baby's gone too.

She sees them outside the 7-Eleven as she turns the corner: Nick with his hands in his windbreaker pockets, shivering; the baby's head bobbing slightly in his stroller, his eyes flaming. Nick is panhandling, telling passersby he needs to buy milk for the baby. A child tugs at her mother's jeans, and the mother rummages in her purse for change. The child hands the money to Nick and the baby smiles. An older woman walks by and shouts at Nick. She gave him enough money for milk twenty minutes ago. Why won't he take the baby home and feed it? Then Nick sees Aura but he doesn't move. Her stomach twists and she turns around and heads back to the apartment. She lies on her side underneath the grinning crocodile and the bored woman, and hugs her knees. She feels numb.

Nick brings the baby back half-an-hour later.

"Asshole," she hisses.

The baby teethes and drools on the giraffe's rubber neck. Aura writes songs. She doesn't want to be like Courtney Love anymore. She'd never have plastic surgery, or shop at Versace, but someday she'll be on the cover of *Rolling Stone*.

One day she goes out walking with the baby and when they get back the stereo's gone. She's in the bathroom when Nick comes home, filling the basin with water and balancing the naked baby on her hip. Nick's out of his head, but when he holds out his arms she gives him the baby. He rubs the baby's back and kisses him. Aura tests the water with her wrist, turns back to take the baby and sees Nick sway. She sees the baby slip through his arms and she's reaching out but not fast enough. The little naked body arcs over and falls, head first, and she can't catch him although it takes so long for him to reach the floor, and there's the unbelievable thud of his head on tile and then dead quiet until he finally screams.

And Nick is holding his hands up in front of his face, shaking his head as if he has water in one ear, and the baby is the only one able to cry.

The girl from across the street says, "Hey, little guy, what's up?"

Aura takes a deep breath. "He had a bad fall a couple days ago. He fell on his head." She has no idea why she's saying this. She can't remember when last she strung so many words together. Her voice sounds thin and her tongue feels swollen.

The girl gapes at her.

Aura says, "His father dropped him. It was an accident. He didn't mean to." She thinks, *Now she hates me.*

The girl sighs. She squats on the sidewalk and takes hold of the baby's feet. After a few minutes she says, "One time when I was five I thought my mother was dead." She looks at the baby's feet when she says this. "She was lying in the middle of the floor and my little brothers were shaking her and poking her and she didn't move. When I picked up her arm it just flopped back down, so I called 911 and told them she was dead." She swings the baby's feet one at a time, up and down, up and down. She draws them apart, then brings them together. Open. Closed. Open. Closed. Then she looks up at Aura. "He's going to be okay, right?"

"We don't know. He's okay now, but the doctor says there could be problems later. Sometimes it takes years before you find out there's damage." Aura looks for a cigarette, lights it, exhales. "Because babies have these soft spots, you know. On their heads."

The girl says, "I know."

Nick hasn't come home for over a week but there's the smell of him on the pillow and his T-shirt's still balled up under the sink. The crocodile and the woman over her mattress are smudged. There are times when she hears the baby but feels too heavy to move, and then he cries until he drags her from sleep.

Nick hasn't come back since the day he dropped the baby, and when the baby fusses Aura jiggles him and pats his back and whispers, "Hush." Once or twice she pats too hard, or puts him down too roughly, or gives him a little impatient shake so that he stares at her, stunned, then gasps and howls. She holds him and shivers and remembers how Nick sat on her when he cried at night, and what would she have done to the shuddering rag-doll body if he hadn't? She holds him close, kisses soft downy scalp where bone has not yet fused; she nuzzles the small shell whorls in his ears and whispers, "I'll get you a better life."

Some day she'll be under coloured spotlights, the audience roaring, arms waving high, their lighters blazing like floating stars, and she'll dive right off the edge, she'll fly over the surge of outstretched hands.

She smokes cigarettes down to the filters and wishes she could get high and thinks, *He's not coming back, not ever.* She hugs the baby and says, "You can't count on anyone in this life."

When she closes her eyes Nick is lurching with the baby, he's blacking out, and she can't forget that slow flip, the baby dropping headlong, the sickening crack of head on floor and how long it takes until he cries. Nick swaying, shaking his head, not remembering, but she'll never shake it away. He hit the ground, bounced, landed on his back. That slow headlong tumble, endlessly replayed. That thud. She puts her hands over her ears, squeezes her eyelids tight, Christ, her baby falling like that. The heart-stopping moment of no sound, until breath returns and the crying starts.

Across the street the girl stands on her porch and the trumpet takes her breath and flings it wide.

# TIMOTHY TAYLOR

# Francisco's Watch

In 1955, my father left the St. Andrew Jesuit Noviciate in Poughkeepsie, New York to pursue a non-monastic life. At this pivotal moment, as he turned away from becoming a Brother just days before he would have pledged eternal vows of poverty, chastity and obedience, his mentor Brother Francisco gave him a watch as a blessing and a personal gift. Francisco was originally from Madrid, blind and stooped, and the watch suggested that he supported the difficult decision my father had made. It was a tacit statement of support but one that my father wore on his wrist as if it were a written endorsement.

My father told the story often.

"Nicholas." Brother Francisco came tap-tapping into Dad's room with his whited-out eyes on the perpetual horizon and a gaunt hand extended, something gleaming on his wrist. "Here, Nicky, help me off with this." He held my father's shoulder for support, reaching up to do so. Dad was a big man, full name: Nicholas Lacroix. French angles and a handsome jaw line. A monk that got the eye. A monk now poised to do a range of un-monk-like things including a decade in New York painting and, some years later, an ill-fated K-2 siege climb during which he broke both wrists.

"A watch? Brother...." Pretty golden ring around a bulging crystal. Lizard strap. There were tiny red date numbers, from one to thirty-one, etched around the very perimeter just outside the hours.

"I know, I know." Brother Francisco was saying. "Put it on. It feels good doesn't it?"

It did. Hefty.

"1934 Movado Triple Date. Do you know Movado? Founded over 100 years ago in the Jura Mountains of Switzerland at La Chaux-de-Fonds by Achille Ditesheim. Now, while we wait here and listen for the footsteps of time, you will watch minute by minute as each one approaches. You will see it come around the bend, watch each second sweep into sight and then run by and into the past.

That will be something for you Nicky."

"Well, well." Dad was still stunned. Staring at his wrist. "Look at this."

There was a kiss on both cheeks. Then the blessing. Brother Francisco leaned his cane against the bed and took my father's wrist in his hands, one palm covering the watch.

"Oh Father," he said, "No man may know the hour, but Nicholas Lacroix will now, at least, know the hour."

Jesuit monk humour, I always thought, although my Dad told the story straight.

I took it to a jeweller years later. I had just turned 38 and I was painting in my studio on a Tuesday afternoon. Checking the time on my wrist, idly, I was swept with my memory of this story and, acting on impulse, I cleaned up and walked across town to Egbert the German Watch Man.

Egbert worked out of a serious, tiny, precise shop on Homer Street not far from my studio. Opening the door you had to watch not to hit Egbert the German Watch Man, who may or may not be hunched over his work bench, staring down the workings of a petulant Patek Philippe. To remind customers of this and to provide himself with a warning in the event they forgot, Egbert had a little bell rigged to the handle and a sign that said: Open Most Carefully.

"This is a nice watch," Egbert muttered as he looked down at Francisco's Movado. A flop of hair was thrown down from the top of his head, almost to the green velvet desk, as he focused in with his monocle.

"This is a very nice watch," he repeated. He turned it over, reading it first with his fingertips. And then, he clamped a silver wrench to the hexagonal back piece, twisted firmly in a single soft motion and exposed the mechanism.

"Where did you get this watch?"

Egbert let a vaguely accusing silence hang in the little room as he gently probed the workings. "See here," he said without waiting for an answer, without lifting his head, indicating with a tiny steel screwdriver something I presumably couldn't see without a microscope. "It says here: "No man may know the hour but Nicholas Lacroix will now, at least, know the hour.""

Egbert looked up at me and let his tubular black monocle fall from his socket to the end of the beaded chain alligator-clipped to the collar of his white cotton shirt. "What do you suppose that means?" he asked me.

"Nicholas Lacroix was my father," I explained.

"I see," he said frowning. "He is dead now."

"He died, yes," I said.

"Did he know the hour I wonder?" Egbert looked down again at the watch. Then slowly, gently, he re-assembled the pieces. "It needs no cleaning," he said. "It was cleaned in New York City in 1954 and is still very clean."

I raised my eyebrows.

"Inside here," he explained. "Old jewellers used to make a mark just inside the cover. Date and place of cleaning. Marked at the same time as the engraving I should think."

I took it back and strapped it on.

"You want to know what it's worth." Egbert then stated. I shrugged. It was true, I did.

"It's worth between $500 and $1000 dollars," he said.

"That much?"

"If you sell it to me," Egbert went on. "I would pay you maybe $500 dollars. But if you came to me to buy one, then I would look around for you and you might have to spend as much as $1000 when we found one. This is a rare watch. Take care of it."

I left Egbert's shop, his bell tinkling its little reminder to be most careful.

Then I walked slowly back to my studio with my precious watch which had travelled from the Jura Mountains of Switzerland to a shop in Barcelona. Into the collection of Count Teo de Castillo. From there, upon the Count's death, to the wrist of his son, Almo de Castillo, who became in time Brother Francisco. From Brother Francisco to a drawer under his bed in the St. Andrew-on-Hudson Jesuit Noviciate in Poughkeepsie, New York. From there, by way of a propitious decision and a generous gift, to one Nicholas

Lacroix. Newly minted as a civilian, as a man with ambitions and a sense of the time before him. Who would wear Francisco's Movado in New York as he experimented with (among other things) Pop Art. The same Nicky Lacroix who would much later have one small successful show, a series of twelve fire hydrants all of which, the story goes, were sold to the newly famous Andy Warhol.

The watch came to me eventually, in a padded package from an estate lawyer in upstate New York.

To me. Painter. Royal fuck up.

"Come in," I said to her.

We went to cheek-kiss, as had long been our practice, but she turned her head just slightly and we half lip-kissed.

"How did you get home?" she asked me, pushing her red hair off her forehead.

I was distracted that afternoon by large events in my life and walked away from her, across the studio and stood by my window looking down into Hastings Street, watching the drug dealers.

"I lost my father's watch," I said to her. "I just can't believe it. It was the only thing he left me." This was the first time I had spoken about it since I had discovered the loss that morning, and it became more real to me having stated it aloud.

I turned back into the room. She stood squarely in the middle of my painting area, a thin girl with long legs and a light pink complexion whom I have used as a model at various times over the years. The previous night I slept with this thin girl, my model, and her slender ankles crossed one over the other in the small of my back. Today, my wife Gillian would return from Toronto where she had been engaged in business, which I understood to be worth millions of dollars.

"I am so sorry David," Sophie said to me. Her hand dropped resignedly to her side and she came across the room and sat in my fan-back chair, flopping down into it, her legs extended. "Where do you think? In the cab? At Café de Paris?"

We had been there. I remember distinctly checking the time on my wrist between the appetiser and the main course. I glanced at my watch and the robust charm of it seemed meant for precisely this occasion. This rosy presence opposite, the slender strength I wanted to feel under my hands. The ticking time piece marked our certain progress toward her bed, toward the completion of something that suddenly, very clearly, seemed to have been incomplete between us for a long time.

"I phoned. They didn't find anything."

"How about the Casbah?" she asked.

"I walked over. The bartender let me search the entire place."

We had sat together at the front bar in the Casbah. By now we were gently touching one another as we spoke, a hand on an arm or a knee. I don't think I looked at my watch at the Casbah.

The bartender remembered me and helped me look under tables and behind the bar. When I was done I thanked him, and his sympathetic expression brought home to me the barrier which I had passed through. I realised that we were speaking on a new day, a changed day, a day the morning of which had been like no others, my heirloom watch gone. My act of betrayal consummated.

"Lost ads?" Sophie was asking now, speaking up to me from the cushy softness of my chair.

"Lost," I recited from memory. "One vintage men's wrist watch. Movado day-date-time model with black lizard strap. Very great sentimental value. Reward offered. Call David Lacroix."

Sophie's eyes drifted away from me and out the window. We drifted together into silence for a moment.

"I feel terrible," Sophie said.

"In what way?" I asked her.

"I feel guilty," she said sharply, as if I should know from feeling the same.

"I feel terrible too," I said, and it was true, but it was muddled somehow. A less crystalline feeling than I might have expected, I felt primarily afraid.

"And still," Sophie said. "I can't believe I'm saying this but I had a great time. It was nice except for the wrong aspect of it." She shook her head and smiled at me.

I stroked her hair back off her forehead, just as she had done a minute before.

"So what will you do?" she asked me. "What will we do?"

I could only sigh. It felt like the fullest expression of my place and feelings.

"Did you take a cab home?" she asked me finally, after seconds of silence. "You should have woken me."

I had walked the early morning streets for awhile, in fact. Then, when I saw a cab approaching from the distance I flagged it and rode home in silence, thinking about Sophie. I undressed in our bedroom, my wife's and my own. It was six or seven in the morning and I thought I would sleep for another hour or two. I was looking sleepily at a pile of laundry spilling from a square wicker hamper, thinking Gillian would be home by six that evening and that before then I would have gathered and steadied things. Cleaned up the apartment and done some laundry, got the pasta water boiling. I didn't think that I cared deeply for Sophie at this point, only knew that I felt strong, resilient and powerful in the morning having been with her the night before.

I checked my pockets idly at first, wondering in which one I had stowed Francisco's Movado. Jacket pockets, pant pockets. Finally in the pockets of my raincoat, which were all empty.

Left At Sophie's I thought, and then in a tumbling instant I knew that it wasn't there either. We undressed one another. I remembered every detail of it. I had lost the watch before we even kissed a real kiss, before our tongues conspired to touch.

I didn't tell my wife about either event. The one matter was mine to keep or reveal. In this respect our marriage would sit, for a period, like a stone in a catapult. I could leave it alone or touch the lever, send Gillian and me through space to some unknown landing point.

As for the watch, I have several and I simply wore another. It would be entirely unlike Gillian to say, "I haven't seen you wear that Movado in some time." Which of course she then did, a perfect enactment of the glancing, refractory way time progresses in human lives. She'd never specifically noticed the watch in my fifteen years of having it, in our fifteen years of marriage, my father having died weeks following the simple ceremony.

Precisely what she said was: "Whatever happened to that old watch of your dad's? I promised Robert at work that I would tell him what kind you have because he says he wants to buy an antique watch for himself and I went into your dresser and I couldn't find it, is it a Bulova?"

I said that no, it was a Movado, and that I had left it with Egbert the German Watch Man to have it cleaned. The moment I made this statement, I realised that I was a bigger fool and a stupider liar than I'd ever realised before. There were now angles and intersections in my story that I would have no control over and I had needlessly complicated my life still further. I thought to myself, watching Gillian's face, I should be hit by a cement truck. My life should end soon.

I had a bad day, knowing with rising certainty that I loved Gillian and full of the fear of her leaving. Fear that if she left me I would be a penniless, utterly lonely painter without accomplishment, instead of being merely a restless unhappy painter who hadn't captured the public imagination in a few years.

Still, in all this, my head was filled with thoughts of Sophie. Inside and outside me, Sophie swam in my fluid atmosphere.

About the watch Gillian said: "Oh well, when it's cleaned let me take it to work to show Robert, all right?"

"Of course," I said. Liar. Fool. Already lonely.

I was painting nothing of value, not clinically depressed but with a mood between blue and black. I decided to stop everything I was working on, right where I was, and begin a new project: a from-the-ground-up re-appraisal of the nude.

I called up Sophie to see what her modelling schedule was like. We had not continued what we started the night I lost Francisco's Movado, and since a whole month had passed and I had purged myself of compulsive thoughts about her, I had convinced myself that the risk of relapse was minor. It would be nice to work with Sophie again as good friends, I said to myself, even if we knew one another in a different way than friends typically did.

Eventually we talked about the watch.

"Did anyone call?" she asked.

"No," I said.

"It was a Bulova right? They're expensive aren't they?"

I said they were plenty expensive but that no, it was a Movado, considered among collectors to be a second tier maker (under Rolex, say). Still, I said, it had been my father's and before that it belonged to Brother Francisco and thus it had measureless sentimental value. She knew this story already.

"I miss it like a person who has died," I said to Sophie. "There are times I don't believe it's gone."

"I wish you'd find it," Sophie said sadly.

"I look compulsively at a spot on my dresser where I used to keep it," I went on. "I look there every morning as if it will be there. I look, knowing it's gone, and still I look, imagining that it will return by my looking."

"Like the apostles after the ascension of Christ," Sophie said.

Sophie was a lapsed Catholic. It always struck me that there was more Catholic than lapsed about her. To describe yourself as lapsed, however, did provide some ideological flexibility.

"Christ said he would return, and from that point onward the apostles began to look up at crossroads, looking far down the road in each direction just in case Christ was approaching."

"I see."

"It became habit," Sophie went on. "This looking up into the distance at intersections."

99

"They must have made defensive drivers in later years," I said.

"Well I'm sorry, it just reminded me of that. You looking at your dresser for the thing that has departed."

Sophie agreed to pose for me again. The idea was that she would come over every Wednesday for a few hours in the afternoon. At first it was just art, we had straightened out the whole physical attraction thing over a coffee one afternoon.

Then after a couple of visits it returned. I think back and I imagine it coming in the door with her that particular Wednesday, our third session together. After that we had sex every time before working for a few hours. When we weren't together, I found myself again thinking about her. She was on every canvas around me. The parts of her I sketched in charcoal were littered over my easels and benches and across the floor near the windows. The rose stem strength of her. The pink-blood health. When I left the studio in the evening, I took her with me like a hot feeling on the skin after walking by the sea on a cold day. A scrubbed healthiness that only very slowly faded as the hours passed, until I eventually felt only like myself again.

Sophie was over, we were lying on the futon which I have set up behind a divider. The phone rang.

"Oh damn."

"Don't get it," she whispered.

But I had to, in fact. The Ferrell Gallery promised to phone Wednesday and I had promised to be in. Cynthia Ferrell and I had a mutual friend who brought the gallery owner around one day unannounced on their way to get sushi together. They ended up staying for over an hour, looking at almost everything, oils, sketches. Cynthia said she liked what I was doing a great deal. She said the nudes were "confessional" which gave me a start.

I asked her what she meant.

Private, she said. Obviously very personal.

Of course, untangling myself from Sophie's long legs and

wrapping a shirt around my waist meant I didn't make it in time to get the ringing phone. So I waited a minute then checked my voice mail, but there was nothing.

"Damn," I said again. I imagined blowing this chance because I was sleeping with my model and I was filled with a passing sense of self-loathing.

I went back behind the divider, where Sophie was lying so beautifully on the white sheets. She lay with her back arched a little. Stretching her pink length in front of me, not shy in the least. I looked down at her as the phone rang a second time, then I dropped the shirt and sprinted naked across the room to get it. I remember thinking as I gleefully snatched up the phone that I had been given that rare second chance.

"Hello," I said, very cheerful.

It was a jumpy, nervy-sounding voice that said, "Hey is this David Lacroix? David Lacroix? Is this Dave?"

I said that it was.

"Dave Lacroix, you lose a watch?"

"Yes," I said. "Oh my God have you found it?"

My heart, instantly, pounding.

"Where is it? Where are you? I'll come right over to wherever you are." He might have said Poughkeepsie, I would have been out the door.

But instead he said: "Hang on. You got to describe it to me, right? I can't just give it to you until I know we got the right one."

Sophie rolled up on one elbow and listened as I lovingly detailed Francisco's Movado. I painted a picture of it in the phone space between me and the caller.

Movado day-date-month...check. Golden bevelled winder ...check. Bulging crystal.

I think I even told him about the Jura Mountains.

"Right," the guy said, and sniffed loudly into the phone after each detail. I imagined he was holding it in his hand, confirming my description, and the idea of this made me almost insane with happiness. Through the phone lines somewhere, there it was: Alive!

Finally he said: "What colour strap?"

"Black!" I almost yelled. "Black lizard. Not shiny like alligator, more flat black with a greasy texture like boar skin."

"Well..." the man said. "I guess it's yours then."

"Excellent," I said looking across the room at Sophie who was smiling at me. Thank God, the prodigal watch returns.

"Okay, so..." the man said. "Here's the deal right. I don't actually have it on me right now. It's at a pawn shop, but they're keeping it in the back for me. What happened is, I saw it and I knew it was stolen, watches like that don't show up in pawnshops any other way. So I went and checked back issues of the *Province* and I found your lost ad."

He explained how he made a small living reuniting people with their stolen property and collecting the reward. Last week he turned around a Sony video camera in the same fashion.

The man elaborated: "When the pawnshops *know* something is stolen and I can prove it with a newspaper ad, they're happy to use me to get rid of the stuff. The cops closed some places last week, you probably heard they're cracking down."

"Well?" I said. "Which pawn shop? I'm blocks away."

"No, no, no. You can't go in to the shop yourself, these Lebanese guys'll flip."

I asked why.

"They don't know you. Two of their shops went down last week and you might be an undercover cop. As soon as you buy something that they know is stolen, then they're breaking the law." The man took his mouth away from the phone to unleash a series of phlegmy coughs.

"So what do we do?"

"Well I can go in and get it right? They know me," he said.

"All right," I said. "How much will they want?"

"Well," he said. "You gotta realize they probably paid twenty for it. More even."

"Twenty dollars?" I asked, incredulously.

"Well sure."

"That's not much," I said.

My guy paused only a second. "Why? What's it worth?"

"I should get $750 for a watch like that," I said. "Collectors trade the Movado triple date at $1000 if they're really fine specimens."

I saw Sophie wincing on the futon.

My man was coughing and sniffing at the same time. "Okay," he said, recovering, "We won't tell them that, all right? They don't need to know that part. Let's you and me meet. You bring like...say a hundred bucks, that should cover it."

"Just say where."

"There's a church across from the pawn shop," my man said, and gave me directions. "How will I recognize you?"

"Black jeans, white T-shirt," I said. "What's your name?"

He thought for second, then came up with: "Theo."

I hung up and turned to Sophie. "What?" I asked, regarding the wince.

She pointed out the strategic weakness in telling him how much it was actually worth, but I was too excited to care. "I would pay him that much, you know?" I said. "I would pay double to get back my watch."

"Well don't pay more than you have to," Sophie said.

"Hey this is important to me," I said to Sophie. She had irritated me by implying that I should cut some kind of *deal* as I recover this object that had been passed down to me in a way that suggested I was truly meant to have it. Buying back such an object at full price, at double the price —an object that had been mine and then had been assumed lost—was like an honour.

She made a motion as if to zip her lips shut, and I went over, leaned down and kissed those pink, zippered lips.

I stopped at a bank machine on the way over, counted out five crisp twenties onto the ledge, folded them neatly once and put them in the front pocket of my black jeans. Then I found the church where he said he would be and I sat in the darkness for about 45 minutes during which time a single person came in, a crumpled old man who stood in the nave and berated the gloom in vodka breath I could

103

smell from six pews away.

Eventually I went outside. I looked up and down the street, wondering if Theo were watching me.

There were three pawnshops on the same block. I went into one and asked if they had any watches. The man gestured to a case toward the back of the shop. Even though Theo had said it wasn't in the display case, I looked half-heartedly. There were 60 or 70 cheap watches in there, every manner of gaudy and gutless time piece. It depressed me to think of my Movado in such a place. I ached for my watch then, hovered over my own reflection in the glass case.

Another couple of weeks passed. It was now almost three months to the day since I had lost Francisco's Movado and I learned that I had been given the Ferrell show. This greatly improved my mood, which had been deep black since my screw up with Theo. What had I been thinking to tell this Hastings Street rubby that he was onto a piece of hot property he could buy for $20 and sell for $1000? By now Theo would have bought and re-sold the watch and poisoned himself with ginseng brandy on the profits. I tried hard not to think about it.

Cynthia Ferrell used the word again. She said "confessional." "They're luminous, especially the small triptychs. Absolutely vibrating with some kind of confessional power."

The show was planned to include two other painters who hadn't been heard from in a long time. Cynthia's idea was a "What-have-they-been-up-to?" show, three of us who had high-profile starts and drifted out of the limelight for one reason or another. One of the other two artists had been a heroin addict when I knew him ten years before, so I wasn't surprised to learn that some of his intervening years had been spent in detox.

"It takes epochs to recover from the changes you inflict on your own system," he said to me when we all met at the gallery to talk about the show. "But it's a beautiful and frightening spiritual process, that sense of your body and your mind trying to re-construct themselves after you have consciously, wilfully tried to destroy them."

I took Gillian out to dinner to celebrate the upcoming show. I insisted she choose the restaurant, and she chose Café de Paris. We'd never been there together and someone at her work had told her that it was excellent and romantic. And it is both those things, although I might have expected French bistro staff to be a little more discreet. Now a waiter (not even *our* waiter) very clearly said to me as we came in: "Nice to see you again so soon."

It had been three months almost to the day since Sophie and I had been there.

On the way out again he said, "All right. Bon soir. See you soon."

"You come here often?" Gillian said, laughing outside on the sidewalk, assuming the guy was being unctuous.

I probably missed a beat, anyway it was nothing that I said but the quality of the silence I left which held something for Gillian which she then interpreted instantaneously. Not the smell of infidelity or anything nearly so dramatic, just a sense that she had read events and people incorrectly. This is the business person in Gillian, I think. And in this case it meant a sudden awareness that what she had thought was an obsequious waiter was in fact an unusually attentive and smart waiter.

She didn't have to announce all this. I just knew she had changed her mind about the waiter, so I came clean. "I went there with Sophie," I said, but then I fudged the dates. "Just a couple of days ago. That night I came home a bit late, I simply forgot to tell you. She's been such a big part of what's happened here, me getting the show and everything. I thought I'd buy her a bite to eat, although I suppose I could have invited her along tonight to celebrate with us."

I didn't like lying again, but I wasn't comfortable saying we had been there during those days three months before when Gillian was out of town. There was no obvious reason for me to have been treating Sophie at that time and anyway, it was a small lie in the context of all the larger lies involved. Gillian took the final joking reference to her coming out with us and laughed. "No you shouldn't have invited her," she said, taking my arm. "I think she has a crush on you."

So that was that. Well, that and the fact that Sophie broke us back down to friends the following day, which hurt more than I might have guessed.

I had just made a big point of telling Sophie about the Café de Paris story. "I told Gillian we went there after all the hard work we'd been doing, she's fine with it."

That was the moment Sophie chose. "Part of me really does not want to do this...."

I got a little teary, which embarrassed us both.

"Oh David," she said, and held my head, patting my ear.

"You should have a proper boyfriend," I said after a few minutes. It occurred to me that I hadn't thought sufficiently of Sophie's needs in all of this. "You deserve someone who is really yours."

"Maybe," she said, not overwhelmed with the suggestion that a man was her root requirement. "But it's not really that anyway."

"What is it?" I asked.

She didn't want to say. I made her tell me.

"I've been reading about marriage," she said. "Breaking one up is like an offence against God."

This was more of her religio-babble I assumed, which as a rule I didn't interrupt. "How would you know?" I said this time. "You're not married."

"Well I can read can't I?" she said. "And I see it in you. And worse, I see the role I'm playing in splitting you off from Gillian. I'm breaking apart the symbol of your creation."

"Sorry?" I said.

"It's one of the key sacramental implications of marriage," she said. "A human relationship in which there is this fusing, this union, this creation of a new joint entity. Ideally it offers us a metaphoric glimpse of our createdness."

"I don't even believe in God," I wailed, besides which I

didn't think I understood what she was talking about.

"It doesn't matter what you believe," Sophie said. "We're talking about what I believe."

I kissed her a couple of times, the last times. I felt that I loved her and after she left I also felt as if a huge cloud of pain were hovering on the horizon.

The morning of the show I went to my studio to collect myself for the big event. I didn't call Sophie, although sitting in the fan-back chair with my feet on the windowsill I felt the urge. In fact, I almost dropped to my knees when the phone rang. I immediately thought of her and her antique Catholic sense of the world and her God hovering over all of this and I almost converted right there.

Had I prayed (I didn't in the end, I didn't want to miss the call) I would have simply prayed: Please God May This Be Sophie. But without the time for this pitch to my creator, I instead leaped 25 feet across the room and grabbed the phone before the second ring.

"Dave Lacroix?"

I recognized his voice and remembered his name immediately. "Theo," I said.

"You remember me," he said, sounding pleased.

I was angry and yet this was countered by overwhelming gratitude that he had called. "I went to the church and waited."

"Look, sorry about that," Theo said. I guessed he was at a pay phone on Hastings Street, within blocks of me. I craned my neck uselessly at the window, there wasn't even a pay phone in sight.

"What happened," I asked.

"I had to deal with something."

"I bet," I said. The balance was tipping back to anger. "How much did you get for it?"

"What?" he said, sounding genuinely confused.

"My watch. You went and bought it for twenty dollars and sold it somewhere. I'm just wondering how much you were paid."

"Hey wait," Theo said indignantly. "I'm no thief. I

haven't done anything with your watch."

"Oh sure," I said.

"I swear to you," Theo said. "It's still in the back of the pawn shop where I saw it. I went and looked at it yesterday."

"Well what happened to you then?"

Theo sniffed loudly and I could hear voices and street noise in the background.

"Don't hang up," I said.

"All right," he said, "But don't yell at me. This is my time I'm spending to contact you."

There was some more silence. "I won't yell," I said.

"I got arrested," Theo said finally. "You happy? They kept me for a few days, but I got released."

"For what?" I asked him.

"Some bogus crap," Theo said. "So you want me to get this watch for you or not?"

"Yes I do," I said.

"All right, you know where to meet me."

"I'm not going down to that church," I said. "We're not doing this in a church."

I suggested he come up to the studio. I guessed right that he was blocks away, he was exactly one block away on Cordova St.

"You live down here?" he asked, sounding dubious, as if he didn't trust people that came from his own neighbourhood.

I waited on the street outside my building, scanning the street, and sure enough I knew him the second he rounded the corner. He walked into Hastings St. climbing the slight incline toward me, arms swinging widely, gangly stride, ape-sized head with a grubby ball cap on. He had filthy too-tight jeans and a zip-front kangaroo jacket under a jean jacket. Basketball shoes, although not Air Jordans, just a beat up set of Converses that were likely the only shoes he owned.

He came bobbing up the hill toward me, a springy step full of misplaced energy and confidence. About ten yards off he tossed up a hand and yelled, "Yo Dave." He seemed to be in fine spirits.

We stood on the street outside my building.

"So what's the drill?" I asked, fingering the cash in my pocket.

Theo seemed a little nervous, although bouncy. He suggested we go inside.

"Cash transaction," he said. "We might want to get off the street."

There's no lobby to speak of in my building, so I took him up to the studio.

He sniffed around a little. Uttered the same critical comment in front of each canvas. "Right on."

"All right already," I said. "Can we deal with my watch?"

He came over and stood in front of me. "Say the word, give me $100 and I'll take care of business." He was swinging a cupped hand up into the palm of his other hand, smack, smack.

It's not that I hadn't thought about the man's honesty before. The fact was he'd thoroughly convinced me that his sense of truth was more dangerously variable than my own. Still, I hadn't clearly contemplated the moment of transition. The very precise point in time at which the cash left my hand and went into his pocket and he walked out the door with it.

"Look," he said, on top of my concerns. "There's no other way to do this. It's like a drug deal. The cash and the stuff can't be in the same place. I take the cash, I meet the Lebanese guy in his car outside his shop, we drive around the block, I give him the cash, he goes into his store, he gets your watch, brings it out to me, then I bring it up the street to you right here. That's how it works. It doesn't work any other way."

"How do I even know it's there?" I asked him.

Theo shrugged. "I ain't scamming you. This is my neighbourhood. I'm around here all the time. I cash my cheques at that Money Mart over there. I score my dope in the park across the street. I can't be scamming in my own part of town. I'll probably see you next week."

The truth was he looked vaguely familiar. I might have

seen him countless times before. "I don't know," I said. I turned and walked a few steps away from him. "I wish you hadn't fucking phoned me."

Theo didn't say anything, or if he did I didn't hear him. The bastard had me thinking that Francisco's Movado was down there, and having seeded this thought, Theo knew I needed to find out for sure. Any outcome was better than sinking back and trying to accept that what had been lost remained lost without ever having checked. Which meant, of course, I had to fork over the cash.

"You think I'm a junkie?" he said, which I didn't in fact. I thought he was a coke-head at this point. "I'm not a junkie." And here Theo pulled up the sleeves of his jacket to show me his arms. "No tracks."

Theo stood in front of me with the insides of both his arms exposed.

I gave him $60 in the end, promising the balance on his return. I counted out three twenties into his dirty palm. "If you're scamming me, Theo, have a good fucking time with my money, all right?"

I slammed the door after him.

He phoned me ten minutes later. He said: "Well Dave my man, your gamble paid off. He's just in the shop getting the watch now. I'm waiting in the park for him. I'll be up in a few minutes, you have that 40 bucks ready for me."

"All right," I said. It was really too much to have hoped for, I thought at the time, but Theo was going to come through for me.

I never heard from him again.

I calmed down by that evening. The opening was very well attended. I sold two pieces without even meeting the buyers. They came early and left early, snapping up both of the small triptychs.

"You two have met," I said when Sophie approached Gillian and me. This might be the ultimate Terror Meeting for other men who get themselves into my position, the meeting of the two people whose universes contain the antimatter of the other. Mutually assured destruction and all that.

Not here and now, though. Sophie was so sincerely devoted to the sacramental imperatives involved that she had reassured me on this point. "It will be perfectly fine," she had said. "I actually really like Gillian, I think it is totally great how successful she is."

"You two have met."

"Oh sure. Hi Sophie, you look wonderful."

"Thanks, so do you Gillian."

"Well," Gillian said, gesturing around the gallery. "You must be feeling a bit naked at the moment."

"Nobody has even picked that up," Sophie said. "Here are these pictures of me but the treatment is so…personal somehow…so personal to David, that it's really only him people are seeing. Strange, I suppose, people looking at pictures of me and seeing David."

"What are you doing after?" Gillian said, "Maybe the three of us could get a drink."

"I have to meet somebody at eleven," Sophie said, making an apologetic expression. "I almost have to go now."

"What time is it?" Gillian asked me, surprised to think it might be nearing eleven.

Of course, I wasn't wearing a watch nor would I ever again, I had pledged, having been taken by that demonic character not for the watch itself, or for the $60, but for the hope that had briefly flickered around the thought of its return, a hope exponentially more valuable and fragile than the watch itself.

But since I normally wear a watch I looked at my wrist automatically the way one does. And so my blank, hairy wrist stuck out of my suit sleeve naked, where it was contemplated for several seconds by the three of us.

Once again, events glanced off in an unexpected direction. Gillian was struck with a thought; Sophie was struck with a different thought and they articulated both in unison.

"Did it ever get cleaned?"

"Any call on those lost ads?"

Silence.

"Lost ads?" Gillian said.

Here was an exemplary moment in which Gillian's multi-variate world view took on data and slightly re-configured. Sophie wasn't as gifted in this regard, and not realizing Gillian didn't know about the lost watch, plunged innocently ahead along the same track.

"Well sure, from when he lost the Bulova at Café de Paris. I feel so bad that I was with him but we'd been working so hard."

"You lost your father's watch?" Gillian said. "That's terrible David, why didn't you tell me?"

"I did," I floundered.

"When was this?"

Under pressure I could only come up with the one occasion we had spoken of it. "Just after you got back from Toronto, remember?"

"And you were at Café de Paris?" Gillian said shaking her head, then looking at Sophie. Even by her standards, she was taking on a lot of new data. Her re-calibrated model of the situation took a second or two to re-run the numbers.

I gave Sophie a look conveying the data she needed to know it was goodnight.

"You were out with Sophie while I was in Toronto?" Gillian said to me, still standing there in the lobby of Ferrell Gallery.

Somebody walked by me quickly, tapped my shoulder and said: "Nicely done."

"I thought I told you," I stammered.

"No," she said. And then she excused herself to use the ladies room.

"I sold three in the end," I said in the car later. "Both the small triptychs and one of the big canvases. You know who bought the large one? A guy named Francisco. Funny."

Funny indeed. So funny I didn't even think of the loop slowly closing here.

"David," my wife started, and with that she moved us through a wall of sorts. A shimmering wall, a plane of time that demarcated the events that preceded it cleanly from the events that would follow.

Epoch-shift, I found myself thinking, listening to the heavy words my wife was now saying. An epoch-shift described by the dropping away of items that characterized the receding epoch. Not like the shift from Fauvism to Expressionism. Not like the relationship between Pop Art and it's antecedent Abstract Expressionism. Those had been growths, movements onward. Actions that embraced and accommodated new components within revised versions of an old system.

Not like that. Instead, Gillian opened her mouth and formally ushered us into an epoch of perpetual loss, a transition that could not be observed approaching because it did not bring with it any references to the past. Nothing swept around the bend to be either admired or loathed in advance. An epoch merely fell away and was replaced by nothing.

And I had no means to know the hour of its passing.

I have thought on more than one occasion about travelling to Poughkeepsie in New York State, just to view the place where Brother Francisco had worked and where my father was first a Primi, then a Secundi, then re-launched with Francisco's Movado as a civilian. Where his decision to turn away from the eternal vow of poverty, chastity and obedience had been made. It would be worth visiting in the sense that I think of his parting from the Jesuit Order as holy, blessed by Brother Francisco and by the God they both served, the God of whose existence my former lover Sophie remains devoutly convinced.

But I haven't made this trip since I learned recently that the Noviciate moved to Syracuse some 30 years ago. The old building in Poughkeepsie still stands, it now houses the Culinary Institute of America. Perhaps I'm concerned that the traffic of new white clad, checker-panted novices would blot out any sense of the building's original spirit, or that the smells emanating from the once-holy site would mask any epiphany.

I suppose I could go to Syracuse. To the new Noviciate. And there I might stand outside the gates and feed off its vital emanations, imagining the forces that drove my father's devotion and then, while he remained a believer, his quiet turning to secular pursuits.

I might think on the blessing he received, on the watch that was its Swiss-made vehicle.

# The Resurrection Plant

Dad struck oil in 1976 when I was fifteen. "Struck" maybe isn't the right word. More like, was struck by. He read an enthusiastic article about it and became, himself, enthusiastic. This was his way. And so we moved from Halifax to an acreage outside Edmonton, Alberta.

I sat on the front steps of our new house and looked at the dead grass stretching away to the fence by the dirt road, the shrubs lining the drive ready to burst into flames. I was stunned by the heat, by the lack of moisture and colour. I felt like an exile. Marooned on a buff-coloured planet full of hostile, sun-toughened prairie kids.

Mom dealt with it her own way. She was inside unpacking. Not pots or clothes. First, her South American hat collection. Panamas and bowlers. Next, the record player. Dad phoned from his new office in downtown Edmonton.

"Helping your mom, Colin?"

I didn't tell him Mom was lying flat on her back in the empty living-room listening to The Tijuana Brass. Wearing a Mayan bowler. What I did tell him was that I was going to go look for the river.

"Atta boy," Dad said optimistically. "The Atlantic see... it just goes in and out. The river is always coming from someplace, and then going on to some other place."

There were black and white birds that shrieked challenges and followed me from branch to branch part way down the ravine. I climbed through papery grass and some thin silver trees, up over a weed covered berm and discovered the mighty North Saskatchewan.

It was brown. I threw dirt clods into it.

My locker partner was Ted Shuchuk. He had a virgin upper lip, never shaved, which aspired to a moustache and achieved only a faint black smudge that disappeared entirely if you looked at it from a certain angle. His closest friend was a failed eleventh grader everyone called Snowblower. He stored his broken binders, a dumbbell and stray sandwiches on a rickety, homemade set of plywood shelves. Almost every morning I had to brush piles of mouse shit off my books.

Ted spruced up the locker with an Olivia Newton John poster and a Nazi flag.

The gym teacher, Mr. Cartwright, was the first to see the flag, and he cuffed Ted in the side of the head and told him to take it down. Ms. Davison, the drama coach, said hanging up that particular flag was hateful, insulting and immature, but Ted's right.

I waited a week before mentioning it to my mom. She wrote a carefully worded letter to the Edmonton *Journal* and the next day there was a long, if somewhat oblique, editorial about the holocaust. The swastika came down.

"That was my grandfather's flag," Ted said, breathing menthol tobacco breath on me.

"You must be very proud," I said to him.

"Get out of the way turkey, I'm going to work out." And he began pumping his dumbbell right in front of the locker. I had to lean over him to put my liverwurst sandwiches up on that tiny top shelf.

My mom said to me: "He can't hurt you. Don't forget that." It was late September. We were walking through a warm wind on a hard blue night.

After Hitler was gone, my mom emerged from her hiding place in the Black Forest and took a boat to Argentina (this is how she told it). She was drinking hot chocolate on the lower deck, an indescribable luxury, and someone said, "Eichmann is on this very boat!" An old woman, her voice shaking with rage at the diabolical irony of it. And my mom had heard this and been sick: all at once, over the rail, a deep hot-chocolate-coloured, evacuating sickness. Then she fainted, toppling like a gyro and hitting her head on a deck bollard. She woke up wrapped in a horse blanket, her head pounding, and delivered her signature line—in broken English with her eyes still pinched shut: "Damn to Eichmann." My grandmother and the old lady cried. My mom never did. She said simply: "Then we went to Rio de Janeiro, and I prayed for a husband. Canadian or maybe from California."

I have a photograph from the New Year's Eve party at the Canadian Consulate in Rosario where they met. My Dad is flushed and brush-cutted. My mother looks wide-eyed, frozen in the headlights of her own prayers. He took her to Nova Scotia the next year.

Phil Levine wore a black kangaroo jacket and carried an asthma inhaler. We used to eat lunch out at the hockey rink, on the visitors bench. Phil always had a Vonnegut on him, an old dog-eared Dell paperback edition *Player Piano*, *Cat's Cradle*, *Jailbird*. Phil's brother once spent an entire year indoors, reading and underlining bits in his Vonnegut collection, then moved to the Yucatan Peninsula. It was enough to make anyone read the underlined bits. So we sat out there at the rink and talked about fascism and nuclear winter and setting things on fire, until a tanker truck pulled up and flooded the rink. Then suddenly there were hockey players everywhere.

"Goofs with dentures," said Phil, who had a fine eye for details.

We went inside.

"Phil's a Zionist," I announced at dinner.

Scott Miller was not a Zionist, but he knew aircraft statistics and had read half of *Slaughterhouse Five*. Phil, Scott and I ended up in the same science group. Our fourth was Ted. He came over and surveyed his team-mates: "Fatso, nerd-ball and psycho asthma-head."

"You can be Goering," said Phil.

"But I was fatso last year," Scott said, and Ted hit him without even looking his direction.

"Anyone know what this is?" Mr. Duke, our science teacher, stood at the front of the class behind the lab bench, holding a brown crust above his head between his fingers. Holding it like it might break. It looked dead whatever it was. The rad hummed.

"It's a dried dog turd," Ted said, laughing.

"It's a resurrection plant," Duke said. The brown crust

didn't deny this. It was curled in on itself tight as a pinecone.

"And if I said it was alive would you believe me?" he asked, and somebody near the window answered aloud, "No-o-o."

"Well," he said, "how could you prove me wrong?"

One of the girls got it right. "Absolutely," Duke said. "Living things need oxygen."

So, we tried to suffocate it. Duke and Snowblower put it under the vacuum beaker set up on the corner of the lab bench.

"If it still looks the same in a week, what'll we know then?" Duke asked, "Anyone?"

"That it's definitely a dog turd," said Ted.

"What'll we know?" he asked again after Ted had disappeared to the Principal's office.

"That it's dead," I said aloud. My first unsolicited class answer and, in fact, the right answer.

After school, Ted and Snowblower hung out and smoked in the east stairwell. We didn't talk to them. They hung out with girls, knit vested princesses with platforms, pooca shells and three-dimensional breasts.

Phil got moods. He'd walk all the way home and not say a thing.

Scott walked between us, always talking, sticking a hand out on either side of him so we all had to stop and listen to him.

"Someone ask me what the fuel capacity of an L-1011 is." Or:

"Got your jockstraps for wrestling next week? No really, what size did you get?"

After we dropped Scott off at his house, I'd try to draw Phil out.

"Shuchuk's into knives hey?" I said once.

"And flags," Phil said tightly.

"You know he hung it up again," I asked.

"I know he hung it up again," he nodded.

"I could be a Zionist you know," I tried.

"With a name like McCluskey?" He said and peeled off

for home. I waved at his back.

At night we played Ping-Pong and Yahtzee round robins, and my mom and I listened to talk radio. Every Albertan held a personal opinion on whether the Northern Lights made a noise. I saw them a couple times and didn't hear anything. They just waved back and forth and then faded away.

At breakfast Dad read the "Exposed-flesh-freezes-in-how-many-seconds" statistics out of the newspaper. "Ten seconds. Coldest November Day since Nine-Teen-Oh-Too. Says here scientists have proven it's actually colder than a witch's tit. Sorry."

Duke let everyone come up with a way to kill the resurrection plant. Carbon Monoxide, x-rays, two weeks of darkness, chlorine and ammonia gas. By December, I was rooting for the plant.

"Just burn the fucking thing," Ted said, right in one of those unexpected canyons of silence that a classroom will pass through.

Everyone turned to look at him. Duke closed his eyes and clenched his jaw. We decided to put it in a deep freeze until after the holidays.

The bell rang. "All right. The jockstrap hour." Scott said.

The sponge mat was rolled out in the gym. Phil tripped Scott and fell elbow first onto his back. "Body slam," he shouted. They bounced up, tapped into the finely strung mania webbing throughout the room.

"Get off the mat!" Cartwright emerged from the equipment-room. Whistle, stopwatch, green sweatsuit cut like real pants with a wide yellow stripe down the outside of each leg. Red eyebrows the same width as his moustache. Black eyes flicking left and right.

He called me Mr. Vocabulary.

"Ring the mat!" We scattered like ants under a magnifying glass.

"Sutcliffe and Nesbitt," Cartwright read off his clipboard from the centre of the gym glaring around him for silence.

"Sutcliffe, referee's position." Sutcliffe hit the mat on all fours. Nesbitt kneeled beside him hands on Sutcliffe's back, fingers spread. There was silence, I looked up at the ceiling. Green rings around the gym lights were a bad omen. Silence hovered. And then the sound of the whistle was swamped by pandemonium.

"Nesbitt!" Scott yelled beside me. Sutcliffe had done a sit out, sliding out from under Nesbitt's hands and scrambling to his feet. They grappled and fell. All knees and ribs.

"Nesbitt!" Phil and I joined in.

Nesbitt was chest down. Sutcliffe was on his back reefing on a half nelson. Snowblower was chanting, "Sutty, Sutty, Sutty."

Nesbitt's underwear climbed out the top of his shorts.

"Gonch pull," shouted Ted.

And that appeared to break his spirit. Nesbitt resigned with his eyes and rolled. One. Two. Three.

"Who backed the loser?" Cartwright paced the edge of the mat looking at each of us.

Our betrayal of Nesbitt was unanimous.

"I heard some of you yelling," Cartwright said smiling, enjoying the moment, "Some of you, I know, backed the loser."

After gym, Phil and Scott and I sat in the hallway with our backs against the lockers and ate lunch.

"Meatloaf," Scott said, looking depressed. "What do ya got?"

"Gefilte fish and a Ding-Dong," Phil said.

"Very Yiddish Levine, congratulations. What do ya got, Colin?"

"I'm not trading.

"What though?"

"A granola bar," I said.

"All right. Meatloaf for the granola bar." Scott opened a corner of his sandwich, "It's got ketchup and mayo. What kind of granola bar is it?"

"My mom makes them," I said.

"Oh forget it," Scott said. "What else you got?"

"A herring sandwich," I admitted.

"Herring sandwich?" Scott said, "What's with the Yid food guys, how'm I supposed to trade here?"

"Well, I'm kind of Jewish, you know," I said.

We ate and watched the janitor string up red letters that spelled Merry Christmas along the main hallway.

"You spelled it wrong," Scott called over to him.

"What?" he said.

"Your sign is spelled wrong."

He climbed down off his stepladder, wiped his forehead with a rag he took from the pocket of his railway overalls and looked at the sign.

"So how'd you spell it," he said after several minutes.

"H-A-N-U-K-K-A-H." Scott said. So Phil and I punched him until he coughed up a piece of sandwich. Then we went over to Poon's to buy Sno-Jos.

"What's this about you being kind of Jewish," Phil said later. We were standing outside the store squinting in the clear bright sun.

"My Oma and Opa were, so my mom kind of is," I said. "I mean they're not really, because they're Lutheran, but they could be if they wanted to switch back."

Phil took some Wink Sno-Jo into his straw, covered the end with his thumb and dribbled the green slush onto the sidewalk. "Moms pass the Jewish bloodline," he said. And Phil scraped the frozen green pattern he'd made on the sidewalk with the side of his boot.

We went skating in Mayfair Park after Christmas. Dad bought us all new Bauer Supremes. I asked my mom while we were skating, "When does it warm up here?" I had two pairs of gloves on.

"Don't you like this?"

She skated with her bare hands behind her back.

"It's crisp, it's fresh," she said.

The air felt sharp on my cheek for the first while, then I didn't feel anything on my cheek.

"I'm going numb," I said.

"You shouldn't complain so much," she said. And we skated on a bit in silence. It was true that she never complained, not about physical pain.

"Ted hung that flag back in our locker," I said.

She kept skating. The ice was covered with a whisper of snow.

"Phil's a Zionist," I said. Still she just skated. Bare hands behind her back. Ear muffs, no toque.

"I want to be Jewish," I said finally.

Then she stopped, so I stopped. She looked at me.

"What do you want to be?" she asked.

"Jewish," I said.

"No, what do you want most of all. Right this minute."

"I'd like to be warm," I said, without thinking.

She smiled a sort of half-way smile I couldn't interpret.

Then she said, "Well that's not so complicated then. In the spring you will get what you want."

Phil and I planned a camping trip out to Elk Island Park to see buffaloes in the spring. I was talking about this on the way to school and he cut me off.

"I want you to put this in your locker," he said, just outside the schoolyard gate. It was a taped up Birks box. I held it in my glove. It seemed weightless.

"What is it?" I asked.

"It's the resurrection plant," he said.

"No really," I said.

Phil stopped walking. "Do you have to know? I'm asking you a favour. A favour I couldn't ask just anyone. Hide this box in the back of your locker. Forget about it. As my brother, do me this favour." And he took my hand and shook it slowly and firmly, something he'd never done before.

"Well, I don't have to exactly know about it," I said. "Except maybe if it's explosive or flammable. I'd like to know whether to put it on the upper or lower shelf." Phil didn't smile. At school I dropped the box behind Ted's shelves and blew into my cold hands.

"All right," Phil said, grinning, happy. I felt guilty good.

Plus we were late.

"Glad you could join us gentlemen," Duke said.

We sidled in like desperadoes. The room stayed silent after we sat down. No-one was looking around.

"One of us is a thief," Duke said. And I noticed that Ted's chair was empty.

By the time I got out the door after class, and sprinted to the locker, Ted was hunched over digging into the papers that filled the bottom shelf.

"Where'd you put it?" Ted said to me.

My legs actually felt weak. I was hyperventilating. "Behind the shelves," I said.

Ted leaned into the locker. "Oh, here it is." And he pulled out his dumbbell, turned around and started pumping it up and down solemnly.

"You been using this?" he asked me.

"No I haven't at all. I promise."

"Just be cool," Phil said from behind me. He sounded cool.

There was a muscle on the right side of Ted's neck pressing out and relaxing rhythmically as he pumped. I stretched around him to put my science binder away.

"Hey turkey," he said. "I need your notes from today."

"Sure. Where were you?" I asked.

Ted looked disgusted. "Principal. It was nothing."

"What was nothing, Shuchuk?" Phil leaned into our conversation, a big fake smile pasted on.

"Mind your own fucking business Levine."

"No seriously I want to know, I mean, we never talk, you know. How was Christmas, get any cool stuff at all? Guns? Grenades? Gas maybe? Hey nice flag."

"Hey happy Hanukkah Levine, all right?" Ted turned to his locker.

"And back to you Shuchuk. Happy, happy, happy Hanukkah."

Ted was walking away.

"What a pin-dick," Phil said. He was wheezing. He took a drag on his inhaler.

"What's your problem?" I said to him.

"No problem," he said.

"What did you do? What did I do?" I asked.

He smiled, took another drag.

"Take it easy McCluskey," he said. And we walked after Ted down the hall toward the gym.

Cartwright was pacing the circle at the centre of the mat, spinning his whistle. "And now…" he said to the assembled class, "…a special match."

Every light in the ceiling cast a green ring.

Cartwright was grinning broadly: "Will you welcome please, The Snowblower."

Whoops. Ted was on his feet. "Me. Me. Me. Let Snowblower and me go."

Not likely. Never friends. Cartwright's eyes were flicking around the ring. My arms goose-pimpled.

"In the blue trunks…Mr. Voca-aa-bulary."

Snowblower's face went flat with surprise, then hardened into something like sadistic amusement. I stood slowly, trying and failing to hold Cartwright's stare.

"Oh man, that's unfair." Scott said.

"Thanks," I said. "Any advice?"

"The balls," Scott said, "definitely the balls.

"His that is," Phil added. "Kick them, or pull on them."

"Oh, and if you hit him like this, you can drive his nose bone into his brain," Scott said, demonstrating on himself.

"Snowblower, referee," Cartwright barked, smiling at me from behind his whistle as I entered the centre ring.

I spread my hands on Snowblower's sweating back. The whistle sounded far above us and I did exactly as taught. I lunged for his far arm, reaching under his chest, got it, and drove with my shoulder against his ribs. Snowblower rocked a bit and settled. Then he stood up and shook me off. I was hanging from his neck. He grabbed my head. I jerked downward and escaped.

We circled. I could hear Ted screaming "Snowblower. Snowblower." And Scott foghorning away on my behalf.

Then Snowblower grappled, lifted me, and dropped me on the mat. Damn. My face was going to burst. He was working on my right shoulder. I twisted over onto my chest, crossed my legs, tucked in my hands and elbows. My last defense, the Armadillo.

Snowblower was scrambling around my back. I felt one hand on my neck, one on my ankles. I felt his head butt into my side, just above the waist. Phil was looking at me. He shrugged and shook his head. Snowblower was bending me like a bow and arrow, pulling on my head and feet, pushing with his head. I flipped onto my back, a husk, airless. Pinned.

Everyone was shouting. Cartwright helped me up and put a towel in my face. "It's just a nosebleed," he said. I pulled the towel away from my face. The white terry cloth was sticky red in the middle, still connected to me by a slick string of pink mucous.

I got what I wanted most. It did warm up.

Above the dirt-brown snow drifts, the skinny poplars next to the fire station were muscling out buds. There was a mouse population explosion at school. I began losing ground to the shit at the bottom of our locker. There were mice in the halls, streaking for cover in the corners behind doors. Disappearing into the wall under the water fountain.

On a Monday I slushed up the street, the air light and breathable, past sand-crusted front lawns.

Duke came out of the storeroom and stepped up behind the lab bench. He took his time, cleared his throat. Ted not being there didn't even register with me until I saw the blue Birks box.

Conversations slowly stopped, heads turned, seats were readjusted. Phil and Scott were the last to stop talking. I had forgotten the thing existed, and recognized it now like a toy lost in Grade 4 and rediscovered. Like the Bluenose II model in the box in the basement, which I had found before Christmas and re-packed. That I had recognized every detail of, and immediately wanted forgotten.

He stood with the blue Birks box in his right palm. Then he reached over and pulled the lid off and rolled a blackened briquette-sized lump onto the desk. There was no question what it was. Burnt to a nub of it's former size.

We may have doubted, we had all doubted I suppose, but the resurrection plant was now most definitely dead.

"At least we found it," Duke said. "The mouse exterminators were looking for nests in the lockers and...and the person responsible...." His face was a quilt of red and white splotches. "The person responsible has been expelled."

Phil showed nothing. He stared straight ahead, and so I did as well. Scott's jaw was slack. People seemed to breathe around us in unison relief and delight.

The next part happened fast. I went to the locker after the three o'clock bell without talking to Phil. I was thinking of going home. Of confessing to someone or going to the Yucatan or both. And then I opened the locker and saw the flag gone. And something did flush through me. Like I had won something. Pride. Anger.

Scott came up behind me. "You going over to the fire station? Phil's already there."

And when we got into the poplars, it seemed like everyone was waiting for us. Ted was shadow-boxing Snowblower, dumbbell biceps evident under his Edmonton Eskimos T-shirt. Phil stood a few yards away in the long grass, shaking his wire thin arms by his sides.

"This is nuts," I said to him, "This is very stupid."

"And your better idea is?" he said to me.

"We'll get killed," I said.

Ted approached through the thick grass to where we stood. "I didn't burn that fucking thing. He told Duke I did. He's a weasel. You're both weasels. You're both dead weasels."

"I never said anything to anyone," Phil said.

"Fuck you Levine."

"Fuck yourself Shuchuk."

"Right now, man, right now."

"Don't you think...," I started a sentence I didn't have an ending for anyway.

"Hey you're next all right?" Ted said right into my face. He was at one of the angles from which I could see the moustache. It was filling out.

Snowblower was smacking Ted in the arm, bop, bop, get

126

him man, you're gonna kill him. A crowd fanned hungrily around us.

I looked at Phil who gave a shrug.

"Let me have the first go," he said.

So I got out of the way and they did that mandatory circling manoeuvre. I can't say they were really sizing each other up. Ted was doing it for effect, swinging his fist near his waist, his stance open and confident. He was appraising a certain kill, thinking about maximizing crowd value maybe, but at his own speed.

Phil was just waiting. He could have been waiting for the bus. Except his elbows were tucked in to his sides, his whiteknuckled fists trembled at eye level, he was leading left. A useless formality before going out with good form.

The crowd calls for blood became persuasive, even from those who didn't want blood, those who probably wanted to go home but couldn't or wouldn't because leaving at that moment was inconceivable. Girls hopped up and down on the spot. The few junior high school kids there, boys, were pushing each other back and forth, infected by what lay ahead.

"Ted. Ted. Ted." No-one was yelling for Phil.

"Kill him Phil," I screamed. And Phil stepped off his back foot, closed quickly and threw what everyone in the lot must have known was a one in a million haymaker. A sweeping arc. A hate-filled cartoon of a punch with enough power to remove an opponent's head as long as he'd been immobilized first.

Ted didn't even look at it. But he brought a fist up from his waist hard and fast into Phil's throat. A short, blunt movement. Phil's right arm feathered off Ted's shoulder and followed him to the grass. His face was white, his eyes pinched shut, his hands around his own neck, breathing like a stick in bike spokes. Then Ted kicked him in the stomach, a considered, methodical kick. Phil moved his hands, rolled tighter. Ted kicked again. The side of the head. It sounded like: Clack.

Phil rolled away, bloody face in the grass.

"Enough. Fuck." I said and ran toward them. The air was alive with movement. The crowd was draining out of the lot around me.

Scott was crying and yelling: "If you killed him, my dad'll sue." He was on his bike already.

I rolled Phil over. He was bleeding but breathing.

Snowblower came over, "Oh leave him, he's fine."

"You better not've fucking killed him," Scott yelled again, his face red and wet, and then he pedalled away. Standing up for speed, not looking back.

"You later, Vocabulary," Ted said, standing over Levine and I.

"Me now, cheesedick," I heard myself say as I stood up. Clearly I had lost my mind. Maybe I wouldn't feel anything. I felt strong. Maybe I was coursing full of some kind of Judaic adrenaline, making me impervious to pain, to fear.

"Come on brownshirt," I found myself saying. "You want to hit me. Hit me. Fucking hit me. What? Knock me down pussy. Burnt a fucking plant so now you're a tough guy?"

Ted took a step back toward me but Snowblower stopped him.

"Don't," Snowblower said. Ted shook his arm away. "Listen to this little shit."

"Come on, gas me you Ukrainian fuck. Try to kill me Eichmann."

"Oh, I'm going to enjoy this," said Ted.

"You want Duke to come out?" Snowblower had Ted by the arm again. "Let's get out of here, man."

"Bastards took my flag, let me kill him," Ted said.

"Come on Eichmann, I'm not fucking afraid of you," I said.

"Leave the girls here," Snowblower said, almost softly.

They walked out of the lot, Snowblower pulling Ted through the grass. I wanted them dead.

"Anytime," I yelled after them. I was delirious.

But they didn't come back.

"Nice work," Phil said. He was sitting up behind me

holding his throat and laughing. It looked painful. He had to go into his Adidas bag and get out his inhaler before he could speak again.

"Eichmann?" he said, wheezing, bleeding, laughing. "Fucking Eichmann."

Then Phil reached into his bag again, took out the resurrection plant and handed it to me. I had never felt it before. It was crumbled, a little worse for the wear. Tender to the touch, like dried cedar. But all there. A tough little plant. Completely unburned. As alive as ever.

"Just do something with it. Anything." He said to me.

"I thought this was burnt. What's that in the school," I said, confused.

Phil winced and strained some blood through his teeth into the grass. "A pine cone. A burnt pine cone," he said finally, coughed, spit some more. Laughed another painful laugh.

"Jesus." I said. I felt light, and I sat down suddenly, then laid back in the grass. The sky full of horsetails.

I kept the resurrection plant for three days before I talked to my mom. Even then I didn't tell her anything, only that I had something that wasn't mine. She said: "Is it from a store?" And then when I shook my head she said: "Does it have a proper owner?"

I said that its real owner thought it was dead. And that made her think for a minute. "Then put it where it belonged before its real owner even knew it was alive."

Of course it only needed water. I carried the resurrection plant down into the river valley. I found a spot near the sludgy bank. Buried it halfway in the moist brown soil, full of bugs and worms. The bowl-blue sky held out space above me. And in less than a week there was a fist sized bush that sprang roots and pushed itself deep into the prairie.

The magpies still follow and fall away, their insults tapering. Their cackles trail behind them as they turn back toward the highway, toward road kill and other concerns. The papery grass still catches in my cuffs and laces. The muddy bank gums my leather soles.

I kneel. It has grown as high as my chest.

I hold the branches, which I think smell of musty pine and pepper. The branches aren't dry. Aren't lifeless. They're full of the earth's moisture. Full of the water that the earth holds from the air. Moisture churned by beetles and fertilized by generations seeking to be reborn.

# Copper Cliff

I knew a man who bought a house in West Vancouver on the North Shore of Vancouver's Burrard Inlet. He paid $30,000 for the house in 1963, three times the money he made in a year at that time, most of it borrowed. The man was a biologist.

The biologist's house was in a neighbourhood called Copper Cliff. The neighbourhood was new, although not in the way we think of today: planned sub-divisions set down in a grid of streets, fully plumbed and wired. In fact, people from Vancouver had been coming to Copper Cliff since the turn of the century, First Nations for many hundreds of years before that. But until the Guinness family built the Lions Gate Bridge in 1938, Vancouverites came here by water. It was cottage country and the original houses reflected this fact: shingled, porched, with stone chimneys and just a few rooms each. Even after the bridge went in and the Guinness family began selling lots in the swanky British Properties, this neighbourhood stayed remote for several more decades. The westernmost fringe of West Vancouver, itself distant from the City of Vancouver proper. A place at several removes. There was a Copper Cliff sign carved out of cedar logs, but no sidewalks, no streetlights. The houses were separated by stretches of forest, an overgrown playground of salal and Douglas fir, dogs, rusting Volvo station wagons and kids.

These kids were a bit wild. They spent their summer vacations on the cliffs that gave the neighbourhood its name, eating huckleberries and smoking rolled up tubes of Arbutus bark harvested off the trees. They would have had no idea that their presence here was a new thing or an old thing, or that the stubby white posts pounded deep into the dirt in various obscure places through the forest were actually survey monuments, markers for empty lots. It would have been puzzling to think that this forest had been measured for any purpose. Unsettling to think that the cottages would ever be gone, replaced by the houses of famous artists, yacht designers, one rock star (ageing) and one Bruneise prince (disgraced).

Of course, the kids weren't puzzled or unsettled by any of these things because, at the time, nobody knew.

The biologist didn't know either. In 1963, he was studying salmon migration and spawning behaviour and was newly married. His wife became pregnant and they wanted a house. Every dollar they had plus what the local bank manager would lend them came to the asking price for 515 Arbutus Crescent (legally: Lots 25, 26 and 27, District Lot 347, City Plan 82, Municipality of West Vancouver). A pretty cottage at the very end of the street, on a spit of Copper Cliff that jutted out above a dense forest of Douglas Fir and which had a broad view of Howe Sound beyond. They offered the asking price to a bare-foot woman whose children were grown and who was moving to Saturna Island.

Some months later, the man's wife had a baby, born on the living-room floor of the cottage. A winter baby, a boy. Premature, neighbour/midwife presiding. And when the boy was old enough to journey outside on his own, the world in total—the land, the animals, the things he would learn about people in later years—was introduced to him on Copper Cliff. The boy had a black Labrador named Deemster and a gang of friends with whom he captured salamanders, made slingshots, killed crows and garter snakes all along the cliffs, through the forests and years of his childhood. They were linked—the place and that boy—coupled through his parents, through their joining, through the title on which both his family name and the property's long legal name were written.

If anyone had been paying attention, if anybody had been interpreting the signs they might have fingered the American artist as the lead indicator of changing weather systems. He came around the time of Khe San, left when it was safe. In between, he painted 30-foot canvases on a massive easel erected among the trees in his backyard—the obese nude in powered water craft was his unswerving artistic imperative.

Gone, his mark remained. His house of cedar timbers—*a longhouse-igloo cross*, he once told the biologist, *the quintessence of this refuge nation*—had opened a wide gap in the dense fir that hemmed in and protected the bluff. And through that breach the flow began. The yacht designer and the rock star came. They tore down the cottages and built their own houses. They cleared openings in the forest for a view of the trees and the water beyond. New mailboxes sprouted in the dirt where the sidewalk should have been.

When the disgraced prince arrived, he brought with him an architect, a landscaper, a lawyer, a mistress and a wife. His house took six months to build. A marvellous time for the boy and his friends, who would rove the construction site after the work crews were gone for the day, climb the scaffolding, kick over toolboxes, steal scrap timber for their tree forts. A time punctuated notably in the fifth month, when the boy stepped on a nail coming up out of a length of two by four. The nail pierced the ball of his foot just behind the toes, drove up between the bones and clean out the top of his sneaker.

And when it was finally finished—even if you had been unimpressed by the artist's igloo longhouse, the yacht designer's Eriksen—the Prince's house could bring you to a standstill walking down Arbutus Crescent. A seventies-era expanse of expanses: polished concrete and glass. Like an alien craft had descended from the night sky and burnt out its own place in the forest. No lawn. Many many skylights. In the back yard there was a 2500 square foot pool into which the kids once pissed, in the middle of the night, yellow arches refracting moonlight from where they stood on the granite outcropping where the squirrel graves had been.

The biologist took no notice. He built his hatcheries and sent his fish out to sea. Each year, reliably, these cultivated fry mingled with wild fry, matured, were caught in their millions or escaped harvest to find their way back up a thousand streams to spawn, to die. The biologist lived in the submarine silence of a misconception: that human technicians would strengthen a natural system. That the sins of the fathers would not be visited on the sons.

Time went by. Ocean temperatures rose, mackerel migrated north and predated on salmon in places they had never in history predated before. Hatchery stocks strengthened. Other streams died, or were paved over, or made into tractor highways for logging camps. Robust stocks mingled at sea with weak stocks. There were too many boats. There were too many users. There were outstanding, unsatisfied claims from the not-deep past of unsigned treaties and overtly broken promises. His son was long gone, his wife not well. The cottages had all disappeared except for his, lonely on its high cliff, looking out over the questioning sound.

He retired.

He was having breakfast one day, our biologist. A widower sipping Metamucil and eating a muffet. The phone rang. And by answering it—like his son's first steps outside the front door those 30 years before—the man was introduced to a new world. Only in this case the details of its utterly changed landscape and the new things that had to be understood about its people were introduced to him by a real estate agent.

He could not have anticipated that what had once been his for all the money he could gather together at one time could now only be had for all the money he had ever earned in his entire life lined up end to end.

"All the money you have ever earned," the real estate agent said. "Imagine every dollar you have ever earned and spent...unspent again."

On the phone to his son, a few years later, the father made a passing reference to the tree in front of his Phoenix condominium complex, a monkey pine. To the son, his comment slammed home an image of the arbutus. Of the bark. A tinder dry smoke you never once inhaled without coughing. He remembered forgotten friends, wet forest, huckleberry. Deemster daydreaming on the moss, cliffside, the picture of canine peace and certainty.

"Do you miss it?" the son asked. "Copper Cliff? Ever?"

There was a perplexed silence from arid Phoenix.

"And your work?" the father asked. "How goes your work?"

Badly, but I didn't tell him. He spoke in a voice I hardly recognized. A mechanical wheeze forced around the nosepiece of an oxygen unit he pulled behind him on a two-wheel cart. This fate imposed on a man who never smoked. My father didn't need to hear *badly*.

Badly how? He would have asked.

Badly, I would have been forced to answer, insofar as I was just fired. As in: I am leaving Vancouver, going into hiding.

I got an email from my boss, Talbot, telling me about the meeting. I went downtown, rode up 22 floors to the boardroom to face a table-full of people I hadn't expected. The Vice President of Talbot's group, a Palo Alto gun named Linster, was there. More ominous still, a crew of people from the client's office. Not just Vancouver, but Victoria. The Director of Land Titles, appointed by the Attorney General himself.

I took the chair that had been left vacant for me, the one nearest the door. I pulled the chair out firmly, without fear, took a seat and looked up the long table at each of their faces in turn.

Two Assistant Deputy Registrars from the Vancouver office asked the questions. They tag-teamed. They wanted explanations for everything. Many things they didn't understand and I would explain carefully, often repeating myself, expanding and clarifying. Real detail stuff. Password conventions. Access protocols. Trespassing logs.

Linster watched me the entire time, emotionless. Talbot sat with his arms crossed, face furrowed and eyes locked on the table in front of him.

The Deputy, meanwhile, listened for a full hour, didn't say a word. Hour two he cut off one of his Assistant Deputy's mid-sentence and asked a question of his own, which he presumably felt was a zinger. A silver bullet to the heart of the matter.

"Adam, simply put...." Then he stumbled on the word

he did not want to say, or pretended to stumble. "Have there been...*hackers?*"

I told him no, truthfully.

"A virus?"

We had covered this area, of course, but no.

"But it doesn't work, does it?" the Deputy said, speaking very slowly. "At the end of the day...if we tried to run this system tomorrow or next week, even at month-end as scheduled...we'd be in the fire. Wouldn't you say?"

The room was silent. Somewhere, somebody was sharpening a pencil with a little hand-sharpener. Scrape. Scrape. The more they pressed and avoided my gaze, the stronger I felt.

I wouldn't say that, no. I told the Deputy. The weekend test-run....

"How bad was it, in your own words?" the Director asked.

The fucker ran. That's how bad it was. Yes we were sifting through a sea of screwy exception reports. Usage logs for the past six months had gone missing. Granted.

I didn't actually say fucker, although I was feeling invincible enough to do so. I was ice. Teflon. I was bulletproof and my words were dumdums. I was the rushing tide, baby.

I said *pop-up flaws.* I spoke of the *archival puzzle.* I promised *strategies to deal with digital discontinuity* (although nobody had asked about digital discontinuity). I warned against *expecting robust performance in complex interconnected environments susceptible to the impact of cascading faults from other systems.*

Talbot was on his feet. I didn't know why he chose that moment, but there he was flapping his arms and squawking and pointing at a carton of print-outs he'd brought with him.

"Is it true, simply..." the Deputy began again. Talbot sat down. Sweating. Red-faced. The Deputy looked only at me. "...true that data has been misplaced...that we don't know *what* is missing yet but that we know *something* is missing. Plans. Records. Tell me if this is true."

Venetian blinds ticked on the glass, riffled by invisible gusts of air.

"Vaporized," I said, suppressing a smile and producing a grimace instead. I might have been passing a kidney stone just as the words passed my lips. "Smoke," I said.

The room was a babbling brook. There was a lick of hard, cold conversational water over a hundred jagged stones. White water. I was answering questions I couldn't hear. Yes, residents in certain blocks of the city did not now, officially, own their land any longer. Yes, technically. Yes, if you looked at it that way. In a legal way. In a record keeping Land Titles Office no personal connection kind of way.

Yes, in a place-less way.

"How the hell did we get here Adam?" Linster said. It was not the volume but the register of his voice that cut through the mounting chaos and found me.

We were staring at one another, quite calmly.

"How the hell did we get here?" he repeated.

It echoed. I might have repeated it myself, aloud, a number of times. I can't be sure.

I left the room.

My office was already packed up by the time I returned there. There was a severance cheque, a box of books and papers and the picture of Deemster I had taped to my monitor. Folded around the cheque was a letter from a law firm—three letterhead names like bullet holes across the top—and in it, elaborate phrases promising my personal ruination should evidence be found that mischief had been perpetrated. Encouraging my co-operation. Promising confidentiality. Discretion.

A sea of lies, but it had its own cascading impact on the complex system of my psychiatry, short-circuiting my manic spiral. Pulling the plug in the basin of my personality. The waters pulled back. I began to descend with the tide. I gave up to gravity.

I talked to my father.

*And your work?* He asked me. *How goes your work?*

I slept for 56 hours straight. Then I packed and fled. The

lawyers' letter confettied the Georgia Straight, distributed by my hand from the promenade deck of the *Queen of Tsawassen*.

*How the hell did we get here?*

Linster could not have known how his words would subsume the others. A loop of encrypted viral logic launched in my boot sector with every other sensation.

I found the Boot Bay Lodge on the southernmost Gulf Island, right down near the border between Washington State and British Columbia. I didn't set out to go there. But it was the ferry's next to last stop before turning around and retracing its course to Vancouver. The last stop would have been obvious. People look for you at last stops, at the points furthest away. Next to last stop seemed inspired, a shadowed place. Protected, I thought.

The lodge was on a secluded acre of grassland and forest at the end of a narrow, crooked bay.

Here, I met Chu, whose parents had owned the place for years. Whose mother was now selling. Chu was spending a final summer here, keeping the lawns cut and the hedges shaped. Doing a little touch-up painting and tending to the rose bushes. She accepted guests if they arrived but wasn't advertising. In the fall she was off to Berkeley, to her last year of business school. She was brisk and ready for the future.

She asked how many nights and I realised I had utterly no plan.

"How many nights are left in the summer?" I asked back.

She gave me the cabin on a weekly basis, for very little. But it wasn't the price that drew me. It was the For Sale sign leaning over in the ditch next to the front road, supported by the split-timber fence, covered over with long weeds that might well have been cleared.

"Forty nine," she said, opening the windows of the cabin and helping me make the bed.

"Forty nine what?" I asked, feeling again, the delicious desire for sleep.

"Forty nine nights left in the summer," Chu said.

I was alone for awhile after that. A week or ten days. Then Chu came knocking. It was noon, hot out. She was wearing her bathing suit and carrying a wicker bag full of towels and gear. She was taut and small. Fit and rounded. Health itself.

"Nice out," Chu said, pointing to the sky. Staring at me. I had been lying on my bed. Smoking.

"This is a snorkel," she continued, pulling a plastic tube out of the wicker bag. "This is a mask."

"Oh yes," I said.

"They enable us to go underwater," she said.

Startling in its newness, this zone Chu showed me. So long had I floated on the variable surface. And here was a sun dappled place of almost complete silence.

I wasn't very good at it. I paddled, I dove. I panicked at depth, suspended, contemplating my empty surroundings, as the words came through the water from a great distance. *How the hell did we get here?*

Those staring faces at the boardroom table were reflected in the broken shells on the sea floor around me, the dawn of their belief in something they did not want to believe. Linster's clear certainty. And then I would be kicking back toward the sunlight above. Tearing off my mask and gasping on the surface, looking over at Chu sunning on her favourite rock. She would glance up from the *Report on Business*, shake her head and smile, serene while the summer drained away around us. Me with salt water and tears streaming down my face. The emblem of displacement.

The last weekend of the summer, the black Lincoln Navigator arrived.

I had finished my swim and shuffled off the beach, up past the red tide warning signs, through the orchard toward my cabin. I was running a hot shower, looking out through the window above the toilet, and I saw the huge black sports utility pulling up in front of the big house.

Chu's cousin, I thought. A lawyer. The only person I

knew she was expecting.

I showered, scrubbed myself free of salt water. I sat on the end of the bed afterwards and closed my eyes, trying to find that place in-between, neither soaring nor despondent. Free of thoughts. A place where life idled along as it did for dogs as they day-dream. I thought of Deemster.

Chu came looking for me. She knocked on the cabin door with her *Don't Pretend You're Not In There* knock. Boom-Boom, with the knuckles. She had another knock composed of tight little triplets I had come to know. Tic-Tic-Tic, with the nails. I thought she probably wanted her black sweater, which I was sitting on at the moment.

She needed a light, in fact. When I opened the door, she was standing with a woman who was holding a pair of barbecue tongs. "You cannot barbecue without fire," the woman announced.

Lisa. Chu's cousin the lawyer, as I had guessed. She had a reedy figure and a large symmetrical face. She shook my hand very firmly.

After I'd found a pack of matches, they lingered, chatting about not much. Lisa stood flipping the matches over and over in her thin, powerful hands.

"Smoke?" I said, when it came to me.

Lisa broke out a wide smile.

"You quit," Chu scolded.

She was starting again, apparently. "Everything is going to be different from now on," Lisa said. She lit her smoke and held up the flame to mine.

Then, after a deep drag: "*Sic Transit Gloria Mundi.*"

They laughed and continued talking. I went out onto the front step and looked up through the trees toward the Navigator. A man was unloading bags from the back. He matched the vehicle, you might say. Dressed in black, with a sleek, silver head of hair and a craggy, all-terrain face. The expensive-go-anywhere combination that was ubiquitous these days, the look that explained the popularity of Rolex watches. He was humping gear up to the front porch of the lodge and inside. Two heavy black nylon gym bags. Then, two more identical bags that he carried very carefully, looking both directions before opening the screen door as if anticipating how he might be ambushed.

When she left, Lisa waggled the tongs at us and said: "Steaks at seven."

Chu stayed back with me. She was looking down at my unpacked duffel bag in the closet. I was sitting on the bed again, enjoying the recalled image of her standing naked in the open bathroom door, brushing her teeth. Feet planted. A hand on the back of her hip, fingers splayed downward.

"I could go with you," I said. It slipped out. "I could find work down there."

Chu came over and stood in front of me. She opened her legs and took a small step forward, straddling my knees. She closed her thighs, reached out a finger to my lips.

"Who am I?" she asked.

A woman. Vital, composed, glistening. Crowned. And when you were born I was on a swing or climbing a tree. I was killing a crow. Ignorant of your birth, where and when it had happened, the anointed time of your arrival.

"You are the mighty Chu," I answered.


Lisa's boyfriend Dexter asked questions pre-emptively. He sounded sleepy, like he didn't really care about the answers, but the questions were there. One after another, some pointed. If you asked anything back, he ignored you. It made things easy at first.

Lisa and Chu were in the house together. Dexter and I were on the deck, sunk back in wooden chairs with big flat handles for drinks. He asked me if I wanted a beer, then produced two bottles of Grolsch and a scotch for himself. We made conversation, waiting for the booze to kick in. "Nice truck," I think I said at one point.

Dexter said he preferred Rover, then changed the topic. "You work?" he asked me.

"I got fired," I said. I told him I did database design, which for most people was plenty.

He was older than Lisa, fifteen, even twenty years. He had jowls. But slick old. Suede loafers, no socks. He wore an ultra-thin gold watch, not the Rolex I had imagined, but the kind made to look like a gold coin and worth more than a car. He had thick-framed rectangular glasses and wore a black wool sweater with a bright green polo shirt underneath.

"Fired," he said. "Why was that?"

"Creative differences," I said, then took a long pull on the Grolsch.

Dexter didn't laugh, just looked out at the horizon, his suede shoe dangling off his toe, then getting sucked back up onto his heel. Swing thwop. Swing thwop.

Then he laughed. There was a 30-second delay, but he apparently reviewed the words and deemed them laugh-worthy. He turned a heavy lidded face over toward me. "Creative differences," he said, quite loud. Then another dry hack of a laugh. "That's about the fucking size of it," he said.

We clinked Grolsch bottles and drank. Then Dexter went inside for two more.

"Doing what?" he asked, sitting down and picking up his scotch glass.

"Database design," I said again.

"You told me that." Dexter looked pissed off for a flash there, like it crossed his mind to cuff me for not keeping up.

I told him that the firm I worked for had been contracted by the Land Titles Office. Searches and Plans. I told him how every piece of property in the city had a legal defini-tion—lot, district lot, plan, municipality.

"Yeah yeah," Dexter said.

"We were scanning in all that data," I said. Every plan, every legal description in the city. Every lot owned by everybody. Developing a single automated storage and re-trieval system. A massive land ownership singularity, data-wise.

Not many people found this topic interesting, so I didn't blame Dexter particularly for showing signs of boredom. I changed the topic for him. Sports talk. Chit chat. We sipped through a few innocent exchanges and then he dou-bled back on me.

"Why though?" he said, squinting around his glass. "Why creative differences doing something like that?"

"Personality conflict?" I tried.

Dexter laughed again, then yelled at the top of his lungs without warning: "What. Time. Is. It?"

He scared me.

Lisa stuck her head out the door of the house, looked over at us both, then withdrew. Dexter sipped, glanced over at me and shook his head with a screwed in eyebrow. When she re-emerged a minute or two later, Lisa was carrying two filet mignon on a white platter that she set down heavily on the shelf next to the barbecue.

"What are you eating?" I asked her.

Veggie burgers, Dexter explained. "The girlies wanted fish," he said. "But the guy down here says your tide is all fucked."

Lisa went back inside. Dexter got up from his chair and started grinding pepper over the steaks using an electric grinder with a headlight at the bottom, the kind they use in steak houses where they keep the lights very low. He stopped once, blew his nose on a red handkerchief and swigged his scotch.

"The Uzi of pepper grinders," he said, pointing the headlight at me. "Gotta love it."

"Fantastic," I said.

"Have a scotch," he said, starting to grind pepper again. "Bottle's on the counter inside."

On my way into the house Dexter yelled after me: "And tongs. There's no goddam tongs out here...."

"Tongs?" I asked Chu, inside. They were in the kitchen, standing together at one of the counters, elbow to elbow. Chu was making a salad. Lisa was putting together a tray of mustard, ketchup and chopped onions for the burgers.

"Hanging on the barbecue," Chu said.

"What about scotch?" I asked, knowing they had been talking before I entered the room.

Lisa showed me the scotch and I went back outside with the bottle.

"Aiight then," Dexter said, who had already found the

tongs. "Let's do these whores." And he flipped the two filets, now crusted in pepper, onto the grill. They began to hiss and spit immediately. "You like rare?" he asked.

I told him medium, thinking his rare was probably pretty rare.

"So what do you do?" I tried. It seemed about the right point. I was nicely loosened up. We had covered off my work (who needed maps anyway). Working for the government (we all do, like it or not). Sports (boxing and the ponies were fixed, team sports were also fixed, but less reliably).

He didn't answer my question. It occurred to me for the first time that Dexter did very few things in life that he didn't absolutely feel like doing. So now, asked about himself and disinclined to respond, he lifted up his head like he heard a phone ringing in the distance. Then said: "Ever been to the Caymans?"

So we talked about the Caymans for awhile. Turns out the chief of police down there is one crooked cocksucker.

I went in to get Lisa and Chu. I walked through the dark lobby of the house toward the kitchen. I didn't mean to do what I did, but my boot actually was untied. I knelt down to tie it and somehow, from near the floor, very still, I could hear that Lisa was crying.

Chu was saying, "Come on. Come on now. What?"

And all Lisa did was cry.

I walked back outside, unnerved. The charred smell of meat and veggie burgers was mixing with the leaf and dirt and salt smell of Pacific Fall. It made me think of how we were all leaving this place in days, for good. How empty it would be then, and for how long.

Dexter was smearing barbecue sauce onto the steaks with a brush.

"Imagine not eating meat," he said, putting down the brush and picking up his scotch.

"They're vegetarian," I explained.

"Oh is that it?" he said. Then he set down his scotch and considered the steaks. "Those two girlies go way back," he told me.

Cousins, I said. Sure they did.

He looked up, surprised, but then remembered. "Yeah right," he said, turning back to the grill. "So about that truck...."

"Sorry?" I said, lost again.

"The truck," Dexter said, looking over at me impatiently. For the second time it crossed my mind that he might be in the habit of hitting people if they didn't keep up. "You like the Lincoln?"

"Sure I like it."

He asked me how I got over to the island and I told him that I'd hitched onto the ferry. He nodded like that was exactly what he had expected. "This is your last weekend, I hear. You want to maybe drive this baby back to the city? I'll pay the ferry."

I was surprised, but it turned out they were taking a float plane up island for a couple weeks to a remote fishing camp. Dexter was unclear on the name or where, exactly. I might have guessed his idea of wilderness tended more to Maui than Masset, but he insisted that he liked catching fish.

"Salmon, shark, dogfish, steelhead trout, blue fin fucking tuna," he looked at me, nodding slowly. "If you can't kill fish, what can you kill. Shit, I've met vegetarians who kill fish."

They had planned to return to the island after the fishing trip. Pick up the truck at that point and take the ferry back to Vancouver. "This way we fly straight home," Dexter said. "It'll save me a trip. I'd owe you."

So I agreed. It wasn't such a hard decision. Chu didn't have a car either. Maybe there would be another couple of days in it for us.

One other thing. "Insurance only covers me," Dexter said. "They see you dropping this puppy off, they'll take a shit. So do it at night."

I nodded stupidly.

"Use the airport drop off. Lock it up, leave the keys on the visor, I do it all the time."

I agreed, again.

"Aiight," Dexter said, satisfied the matter was resolved: "You know, this stuff is cooked. Where the little girlies at?"

"Talking," I said.

"She crying again?" he asked me, but before I had a chance to answer he turned to the house and unleashed another holler: "Dinner. Is. Ready." His words boomed out over the bay, all the way across to the island on the other side of the straight. No echo.

Chu came out first, frowning. Lisa came behind her carrying salad. She didn't look like she'd been crying.

Lisa and Chu had their own parallel conversation during dinner. We weren't talking on top of each other exactly, but if you listened to what was being said across the table you realised it didn't quite link up to whatever Dexter and I were saying.

So when Dexter pointed at his steak with his steak knife and said, referring to the peppercorn jacket on the filets: "El Diablo, good fucking stuff."

And I answered: "Beautiful meat, real tender."

I heard Lisa say: "It really is beautiful. I love the ocean, and the orchards."

Fifty-year-old McIntosh trees, Chu explained.

USDA Prime, said Dexter. From a ranch he owned in Montana apparently.

"Do you fly in your own steaks?" I asked him, thinking about that border, close but invisible in the darkness south of us. Thinking about what kind of person goes to that effort.

Dexter looked bitter for a moment.

Chu's father had planted the apple trees. As a child, she had loved to....

"Business," Dexter said, looking at me like he had hoped he wouldn't have to explain this point. "There is a business in bringing *here* what isn't *here* already. You understand?"

Lisa was looking around herself, imagining the property as it stretched away into the darkness. "It is a beautiful *here*, isn't it?"

"Yes," I said to Lisa, deliberately bridging to their conversation. "It is a beautiful here."

Before Lisa had come out for dinner she had changed into a loose white shirt that she wore untucked. Now she smiled, poured herself more wine and held it up to make a toast. "Here's to here," she said. "And how the hell we all got here."

I clinked Lisa's glass. Chu raised her own with a distant expression. Dexter didn't bother.

"So tell me how you got here," Lisa asked me. "I've heard just a little bit. You arrived on a Tuesday. You were lost."

"He got fired," Dexter said. "Creative differences. Personality conflicts."

"It's boring," I said. Smiling just a little at Lisa. "You?"

"How about our hostess?" Dexter said, cutting off the first word of Lisa's response.

Chu conceded to tell the story. About how her father had come from Hong Kong in the forties. How he had married Chu's mother, Lisa's aunt. How he started the construction company. But she grew irritated as the story unfolded, I could hear, and her pace quicken, her details thinned. She was born. Her parents retired to these islands, to their summer place which they decided to run as a lodge. Dad died. Mom went back to Hong Kong. Now Chu was leaving too, to finish school. To move on.

Dexter feigned interest in the part about school, but when Chu said business school he rolled his eyes. What could anyone possibly learn about business from a *professor?* Chu was forced to defend her studies. Defend school itself. She struggled to turn back the tide of questions and failing, changed the topic. What were their plans, she asked, pointedly.

"They're going fishing," I announced.

Dexter poured more wine, topping my glass right to the brim. "You like that?" he said, gesturing at the wine bottle. Then he started talking about wine without waiting for an answer. About a vineyard he once owned. About the goddam bugs that ate the vineyard. About the moron banker who tried to collect his mortgage after the bugs had eaten the vineyard. About his restaurant in Whistler where he had sold all his wine from his vineyard before the goddam bugs and the moron banker (who probably went to business school)....

"Where?" Chu asked, leaning forward.

"Whistler," Dexter said.

"No," Chu said. "Where fishing?"

At which point Dexter sneezed, set down his drink and pulled out his handkerchief. Lisa leaned over to Chu and started talking about the lodge. About her mother selling. Didn't she mind? Wouldn't she miss spending her summers here? Chu was trying to assure Lisa she didn't mind, but I could tell she wanted to get back to that fishing question.

"Fifty bucks a bottle," Dexter said to me, after he'd blown his nose. "You believe that?"

"Campbell River?" Chu asked.

"Yeah," Dexter said. "Why, aren't they biting?"

Chu looked at Lisa. "Is that near Port Alberni?"

Dexter looked angry. Lisa sipped her wine. "I thought it was Port Alberni," she started, tentatively.

"Port Alberni later," Dexter snapped. "First, Campbell River."

Lisa was back on the sale of the lodge. Were there any offers? How much land was included?

"Maybe we should buy it partner," Dexter said to me.

I laughed.

"Oh right," he said, slapping his forehead. "I forgot. You would be flat broke at the moment."

I shrugged and smiled, thought the comment a passing one before realizing that Dexter was bearing down. Just that second—just as I watched him pocket his handkerchief, sip his wine—just then an idea blew through and he swivelled on me with brand new interest.

"In my experience..." Dexter said, pleased with what had just occurred to him, "...there is always a story behind creative differences and personality conflicts. Wouldn't you say?"

I could smell every leaf in the orchard. Every plump leaf of McIntosh, waiting for October to fall. Chu and Lisa were talking, almost at a whisper. At the moment Dexter asked his question, I heard Chu ask hers. "Lisa, when are you coming back?"

Lisa was looking at Dexter. Chu was staring at Lisa. I was locked on Chu just as Dexter was on me. We were a square dance in a minefield. Nobody wanted to take the next step.

"It was a health issue," I said, finally. "I'm what they call bi-polar. I go high. I go low."

"So were you high or low?" Dexter asked, staring.

"High," I said. "Real high."

Sometimes I got bound up in an assignment. Sometimes, during those times, I would forego my lithium in the interests of riding a little wave of manic energy. Sometimes, without the lithium to narrow my emotional bandwidth, I stopped sleeping. And when I stopped sleeping my body, in turn, lost control of dopamine production. At that point—hardware and software having been rendered incompatible—my control of mood and of the given situation was utterly relinquished. The wave would mount, would curl. The wave would make a pipeline a thousand miles long, never break, just keep on cresting. And I would ride that wave wherever it took me.

They were all listening now. Dexter was nodding intently, face twisted with delight. Thinking, no doubt, of what potential for my humiliation must exist during these times. Lisa reflected something like sorrow. Chu's face only softened slightly, opened. She showed none of the surprise she might have felt.

It lead to misunderstandings, I went on. Bad mistakes or, sometimes, impossibly good ideas that others did not understand.

Dexter held the same demented expression the whole time I spoke. And when I finished, he suppressed a burp, got up and lit one of those porch lanterns that drip wax everywhere.

*How the hell did we get here?*

All the different ways I could have answered the question and I gave a stupid one: "I was raised there."

I was looking at Linster, who had asked this quiet question.

"Where?" the Deputy said, from the other side of the boardroom table.

"Sorry?"

"Raised there, you said. Raised where?"

"Vancouver," I said. "Born and bred."

"But where?" the Deputy said again.

I stopped talking. It was the last thing I said. He knew this much, nothing more.

Lisa was interested by the snorkelling. Conversationally inspired after my confession, I became expansive, describing the underwater world I had discovered. While I talked, Lisa listened and Chu added details. Dexter sank into his chair and drank. Or he paced. Or he stood at the rail and looked out like he was waiting for a taxi.

Chu laughed at Lisa's suggestion that I take up scuba diving. There were tanks in the storage shed I had refused to use. "I don't want air down there with me," I said, gesticulating.

Thirty seconds was plenty, Chu said, smiling.

"Thirty seconds?" Dexter had gone into the lodge. Now he exploded back onto the scene and into the conversation. A tumbler of ice in each hand. "Thirty whole seconds?"

"I get panic attacks," I explained.

Dexter, it seemed, could hold his breath for three minutes. We bet $20. He assumed a meditative position on the edge of one of the deck chairs. Crossed his arms and took a deep breath. At three minutes his face wasn't even red. I went over and held a hand under his nose. Nothing.

"Yikes," I said. He rose to his feet and I pulled out a twenty.

"You put that money away," Lisa said. "He was cheating. Show them Jimmy...."

Dexter was now pouring a scotch over by the barbecue. He stopped moving just for an instant at these words, his back to us. The bottle hovering over the glass, the ice cracking. Then he continued pouring.

I heard it, Chu didn't. She was still trying to figure out the cheat.

Dexter returned with the drinks. He was staring hard at Lisa. "Party trick," he said to me. "Forget the twenty."

Something about the tear ducts.

"Maybe we could go snorkelling tomorrow," Chu said to Lisa.

"We're leaving tomorrow," Dexter said. "Early."

Lisa looked away, then back at me. She asked for a cigarette. I gave her one and lit it. She drew deeply.

Dexter looked disgusted. "Our night for vice?" he said.

"Our night for something," she answered, and blew out a perfect smoke-ring and a smaller one that followed the first. She topped up her wine glass and said: "Our night for transitions."

"*Sic Transit* whatever," I said.

"*Gloria mundi*," Lisa said, laughing.

"So passes something," Dexter said. "I don't know about glory."

"Why you're glorious," Lisa said to him, smiling sweetly. "And quite clearly my favourite client. So successful. So handsome. So...elusive."

"So tired suddenly," Dexter said.

"Not me," Lisa said, taking another long sip of wine. "Besides, nobody asked me how I got here...."

"How you're getting to bed is my question, counsellor," Dexter said.

Lisa sighed elaborately and looked across the deck at him. "Fuck you," she said.

Chu put her hand on Lisa's shoulder.

"It's not a real special story, is it?" Dexter said. "How you got here."

Lisa started to cry.

"Remarkably enough," he went on, voice stony. "It's just like how everybody everywhere got anywhere. By choice. Cold choice."

Lisa and Chu went down to the beach. Dexter and I drank another couple scotches without saying a word.

"So...before they fired your ass out the door..." Dexter said, finally. "Was it a mistake or did you give them something real good they didn't understand?"

He surprised me by remembering my comment that precisely.

"I didn't really give them anything," I said.

Dexter nodded like he understood perfectly.

"Didn't steal anything either," I said.

"Course not. Borrowed maybe."

"It depends who you figure owned the thing in the first place."

Dexter looked up. We locked stares for a second. "You're not sure?" he asked me.

I was sure I was quite drunk.

Dexter looked away finally. Sipped and considered something. "I got my ass fired once," he said, finally.

"No shit."

"An occasion that gave me a chance to learn the Law of Dogs."

"I had a dog named Deemster," I told him. "He used to lie around all day in one spot, up there on the rocks. That was his law: lie in the sun on Copper Cliff and be happy."

Not that precisely. Dexter made a strange face, pushed himself through some internal reluctance and started talking, low and very sober-sounding.

"Understand," he said. "After they fired me, these cocksuckers were going to cut off my fucking head."

I reacted like the choice of body part surprised me. "Why?"

It was a long story that Dexter declined to tell. But the climax, which he cut to, had him running down a darkened alley out in the eastern suburbs somewhere. He thought Port Coquitlam, although he couldn't remember. All he knew is there were bad guys with evil intent driving around with a chainsaw that had been sharpened with his sixteen-inch neck in mind.

"So," Dexter said. "I'm running and I'm running and

these fuckers are chasing me and then I'm in this alley and I'm trying to find a yard I can climb into, a garage, anything. I'm looking to hide, see?"

But every yard he tried—and here he took a long pull of scotch, like a chainsaw he could handle but this detail he found disturbing—every yard had a great big dog in it. And every time he put his hand to a fence, prepared to vault, this dog would rush the fence, barking like crazy. Waking the neighbourhood.

"In the end, I got away, as you can tell..." Dexter pointed to his head, "...but those dogs, they made me think of something. Later. Years later. On an occasion I came to thinking about whether something was mine or not. Whether something had to be stood on and defended or whether it'd be better to just leave the thing and fuck off. You understand?"

I nodded.

"That's when I thought about those goddam dogs. They didn't need a set of instructions to know what was theirs, see? They just knew. And they'd always known."

Dog law.

"The Law of Dogs," Dexter corrected. "Not running around from here to there. Just fucking knowing."

What was left of the porch lantern was flickering in a puddle of wax on the railing. I lit a cigarette. I said: "Who's Jimmy?"

Dexter nodded slowly. "When you drop off that truck," he said. "You look in the back afterwards. There'll be a black gym bag back there. You like what you find in it, you keep it."

I didn't have an answer.

Dexter looked over at me and smirked. "It won't be a fucking head, all right?"

And then, since Dexter suggested it and I wanted to do nothing more, I went down to the beach to find the little girlies.

I broke into the root server. That is what I had done, what I never told Talbot, Linster, the Deputy, even Dexter, who had grown on me in his own way. This act of trespassing gave me access to the plan of every lot in the entire Vancouver area. A finicky process, to be sure, lining up password after password, being forced to start over if I got one wrong. But I got in eventually, and the entire city opened under me like I was flying a plane down the Fraser River at night. The temptation was there, no doubt. To crash everything. It wasn't exactly a delete key away, but with a series of minor hacks I might have wiped clean the legal definitions in the entire database. Pieces of land, parcels owned by people, borrowed and lent against, repossessed and resold, all these might have been rendered invisible. Ownership formally eradicated. A mess that could be sorted out, sure, but a very satisfying mess nonetheless.

I took only the one that mattered. The original, indelible place. 515 Arbutus Crescent legally: Lot 25, 26 and 27, District Lot 347, City Plan 82, Municipality of West Vancouver. There were plans that could be printed out on the plotter, which I did before deleting them and destroying the back ups. There was a long string of digits that comprised the official survey. There was a command to cancel all memory of this number. The command came with multiple prompts along the lines of: are you sure you wish to proceed? And: please enter the supervisor password to authorize this procedure.

I am under the impression that the damage I caused will not be permanent. It will have a life, itself, shorter or longer depending on a whole range of things I do not control. One day the present owner might try to mortgage his house or sell the land. He might die. Then his dependants will learn that there is no title, no duplicate, no registered plans. And if a true copy of the title can't be found in a bank vault somewhere, attached to an old mortgage or lien, then the Surveyor General will again be called and there will be white posts pounded down into the forest around the new house. The land defined afresh.

After we came back up from the beach, Chu and Lisa hugged before parting, rocking together with something

firm and unknowable. Something I imagined was sister-
hood. Then I followed Chu through the orchard to my
cabin. She walked resolutely, straight there. And inside
I started to say something but she put her fingertips on
my lips. The first two fingertips. Then we pulled off each
other's clothes, brushed our hands along one another. Flut-
tered fingers, brailled the skin. Learned more than we knew
before. Forgot things.
 Chu slept. I didn't close my eyes for a single minute. But
I didn't pace either. I didn't have a strange out-of-cycle
desire to drink coffee, or take maybe a half-tab of Prozac or
make myself any more awake any other way. I only lay and
imagined I was floating on a layer of air that covered the
entire world. A layer on which we slid freely, without fric-
tion. And if this layer meant that we had lost our sense of
the stickiness of any one place, I imagined in that bed, next
to Chu, that we all still held onto our grief at this loss. Not
much, but something. A vague and insatiable nostalgia.
 I heard the float plane touch down at four o'clock in the
morning. It taxied into the bay a full two hours before Dexter told us it would. I shook Chu awake and she hurried on
a sweatshirt and a pair of sweatpants. We rushed down to
the jetty but they had been ready and waiting. The plane
was moving toward open water, prop to the strait. When it
nosed into the breeze coming round the headland, the pilot
opened the throttle. The plane accelerated. It hit the speed
needed to fly and left the water in a single leap, just high
enough to clear the trees. Then it turned sharply south and
settled down to fly just above the waves.
 "Hey," Chu said, watching the plane disappear. "Where
are they going?"
 "South," I said. "South as in the US border. As in the
Cayman Islands."
 I told her about the Lincoln Navigator and when we
went to look it over, sure enough, the keys were on the visor. The black bag was in the back. There were two bundles
of American $100 dollar bills. Chu ran her thumb across
the edge of one, but neither of us wanted to count them.
 We went back to bed.

I never saw her brush her teeth again, I regret that. Our final morning together, I woke to leaves humming in a morning breeze, the bed beside me empty. I packed up my duffel and stole the black sweater. Then I went down to the bay and walked along the high water, lapping just short of the red tide warning signs. I waved to Chu, who swam up in a wetsuit and mask.

"We should get going," I said, looking at my watch.

"Let's get the next one," she said, beckoning with her head. "Come have a swim."

Of course, there wasn't a thing she could have suggested to which I would not have agreed.

We crossed on the ferry. I was taking her to a friend's place where she would spend her final night in Vancouver. The next morning she was gone. Driving away from the terminal, I felt her gaze on my right cheek. And I knew she wouldn't have wanted me to turn and look at her, just then. To catch her thinking, even in passing, about the time that was now upon us. A time during which we might miss one another. Even in passing.

So I didn't turn. Didn't look back into that small and perfect, wondering face.

I spoke instead. I said: "Do you want to see the spot where I was smoking Arbutus bark cigarettes the day you were born?"

She said yes, right away.

We drove slowly up the hill from Horseshoe Bay. The Copper Cliff sign had fallen, I would have to guess years before. It was moss-covered and rain rotted. Part of the land again. We slowly reached the crest of the Arbutus Crescent hill, from which point the whole of my childhood universe was laid out before me. The forests had grown back, pulled in tighter around the houses.

"Is that the Prince's place?" Chu asked, pointing.

The moss had crept up all the exterior walls. The space-craft was now an organic thing.

"Is it this one?" she whispered. She was pointing up the drive, through the trees, out to the spit of cliff where the cottage had been. "We should go up and knock. You should say: I was born here! They'd love it, I'm sure."

It was an additional 50 yards, to go up that lane. To round the corner and see what had been built. To return to the site of beginnings, complete the round trip, as it were.

But I didn't. Because it really wasn't there anymore, was it? It was gone. And they were gone. The moments. The units of time that I'd had and spent. The moments that had been given to me, that I had earned or stolen. All those moments were not lined up end to end, up that lane and out on that spit of land, waiting to be returned.

The last time we snorkelled together on the island, Chu showed me a trick. You breathe a little air into the snorkel when you're at the bottom. Then when you come to the surface, the damn thing clears itself. Something to do with the pressure. Fantastic.

And with that weight off my mind, I could breathe more slowly, stay down 45 even 60 seconds. More. We swam all the way back from the sand bar to the beach holding hands. It was so beautiful I would have laughed if I didn't have the snorkel in my teeth. Chu swam us right into the shallows, where the water was full of sunshine and the bottom glittered with duelling crabs and those little fish that dart back and forth and say: "You're here. Welcome. Now just breathe deeply. Just breathe like this."

CHRISTINE ERWIN grew up in Hong Kong and moved to Toronto at sixteen. In 1996, she moved to Hanoi, Vietnam for two years to teach creative writing. Her stories have appeared in magazines across the country, and in 1995 she was a finalist in the Writers' Union Short Prose Competition. She lives in Toronto with her husband and son, and is currently finishing a collection of short stories, *Walking the Dragon's Back*.

VIVETTE J. KADY grew up in South Africa, and now lives in Toronto. Her short fiction has appeared in numerous journals and anthologies in Canada and the United States, including *Best Canadian Stories*, and she has been nominated for a National Magazine Award and a Western Magazine Award.

TIMOTHY TAYLOR lives in Vancouver, and his first novel, *Stanley Park*, will be published by Knopf in 2001. His short fiction has appeared in *Grain*, *Canadian Fiction Magazine*, *Fiddlehead*, *The Malahat Review*, *Event* and *Descant*, won silver at the 2000 National Magazine Awards and been included in *oo: Best Canadian Stories*. Three stories will appear in this year's *Journey Prize Anthology*, and he is working on a second novel.

MAGGIE HELWIG was born in Liverpool, England and grew up in Kingston, Ontario. She edits an occasional litzine and has published one book of essays, a collection of stories and five books of poetry. She has also worked with a variety of peace and human-rights organizations in Canada and England. She now lives in Toronto with her husband Ken Simons and their daughter Simone Helwig.

*Previous volumes in this series contained stories by the following writers:*

*Most of these books are still available. Please inquire.*